Curtain Call

A Vet Detective Mystery

By

Nik Allen

CHAPTER ONE

Jasmine Cline started to reach for the door of her Jeep before turning to run back inside and grab her gym bag. She almost forgot it, and she would need a change of clothes between clients today.

It was a sweet sunny October morning, warmer than usual. The leaves were all golden orange, and just starting to collect along the edges of Hattrick Avenue. They swirled behind Jasmine's old Wrangler on her way to her home office at Merritt Valley Mobile Veterinary Clinic.

Jasmine ran over her day in her mind. Wednesday, October 3rd. She knew she had two home visit appointments this morning. Since Merritt Valley was a small town, surrounded by hobby farms, she and her partner. Claire Gilbert had decided to take their business on the road 3 years ago. It often crosses Jasmine's mind that the success of their business came at a high price to her wardrobe, hence, the change of clothes. She had learned to be prepared with coveralls and work boots. Farms were messy places and farm animals were not polite about getting mud and hay all over her.

Jasmine passed the other business along their block of Grand Avenue. The Muffin Man Merritt's premier bakery was already busy with people buying their coffee and breakfast, the Newsette and Valley View Dental were quiet this early in the morning, and Blackbird, the local ladies clothing boutique wouldn't even be open for a couple of hours.

"Morning, Boss!" chimed Ellie, their office administrator. She was a girl next door type, taller than average, long blonde waves and still tan from summer days spent at one of Merritt's many lakes. She was always this cheerful in the morning. In fact, Ellie was this cheerful at all times of the day.

Jasmine smiled, "Good morning, Ellie. How many times do I have to ask you not to call me that?"

“Probably a few thousand more.” Ellie laughed and handed Jasmine a stack of files. “These are your patients today. Sounds like the Bentons are pretty worried about their mare. Called three times last night”

“Oh, I’ll have to call Eric Canton. Thanks, Ellie.” Jasmine called over her shoulder on her way into her small office.

Jasmine hung her bag up and pulled out her cell. She took a deep breath and chose Eric in her contacts. While she had studied and worked with horses in school and at clinicals, equine medicine wasn’t her specialty. She and Claire frequently partnered with a local large animal veterinarian, Eric Canton. They worked together so often, Jasmine didn’t know why calling him should make her nervous. But it did.

“Hey, Jazz. How’s your morning?” Eric answered cheerfully.

“Hi, Eric. Great. Say, are you busy this morning? The Bentons have a pregnant mare they’re worried about. I’m headed over there to give their Great Pyres checkups.”

“Apollonia? She’s probably waxing. I’m just about finished out at Waverly. I could meet you over there around ten am?” Eric answered. Waverly was a large dairy farm 20 miles out of town.

“Dairy farmers put you to work early, huh? 10 am is perfect, see you there,” she replied.

Jasmine set her phone down and wished she could set aside her nerves so easily. The butterflies in her stomach were harder to treat than any of the pets she’d seen. Eric Canton was handsome but it was more than that. She couldn’t deny the chemistry between them. As a livestock veterinarian himself, he understood her work and interests better than anyone aside from Claire. Though, if she was honest with herself, that’s not at all why she was nervous to see Eric Canton. She cleared her throat and set to work, going over all her four-legged patients’ charts before heading out to see them.

Jasmine checked her medical bag over and replaced a few ampoules of vaccines and diluents. She liked to keep her bag well stocked when she left the office, things often came up unexpectedly. She slid the file case into the bag and zipped everything up.

Jasmine took a moment to look herself over in the mirror near her office door. She didn't wear much makeup to work. Since they were mostly cats and dogs, her clients didn't care, and their owners' never seemed to notice. She was blessed with clear tawny skin and full lips, which were naturally a deep berry red. She had swiped some gloss on them this morning, and a little mascara over her long lashes. As she gazed into her own honey colored eyes. She was glad she had put in a little effort this morning. She smoothed her unruly curls a little but knew there was no taming them. Well, time to get to work, she thought and grabbed her bags.

Her first stop was as simple as she anticipated. Mrs. Murphy's ragdoll cats were treasured and well cared for. Perhaps they were a bit pampered. They wouldn't need shots today, just a quick check-up and some new nail caps. Jasmine encouraged her customers to use small silicone nail covers for cats with a tendency to scratch furniture, rather than declawing.

Princess and Diva were in fine shape and sat nicely for their checkups. The seal point, Princess gave a little fight while Jasmine applied her nail caps, but Diva hardly lifted her head. The sleepy cat glanced over with her brilliant blue eyes from time to time, but Jazz wouldn't be surprised if the cat dozed off.

"Your girls really look great, Mrs. Murphy. Do you have anything to ask me before I wrap up? Any concerns?" Jasmine ran her fingers through Diva's long cream colored fur.

"Well, Dr. Cline," Mrs. Murphy laughed, "How much is too much sleep?"

Jasmine laughed, too. "Oh, I think a few days at a time, with these two. As long as they move around a little each day, I wouldn't worry." She glanced down at Diva, who had, in fact, fallen fast asleep. "They seem to be in fine health. The caps should stay on well around 2 months; call the office when it's time for new ones. I think we'll have red and green for Christmas."

"Wouldn't that be something?" Mrs. Murphy said, more to Princess than to Jasmine.

Jasmine left Mrs. Murphy and the girls and hopped in her Jeep to head over to the Benton Ranch. The leaves were in full color so the drive wasn't a chore at all. Jasmine simply loved this time of year. She enjoyed the view and listened to some local news on her way. There was a play opening this weekend, and a big football game. The Festival of Leaves was coming up next week already; all the local shops would be decorating. There would be vendors and food trucks on Grand Avenue all week and of course the Festival Fair. The Festival and Fair brought in tourists from all over. People came to walk the pumpkin patch, see the animals and farm displays, and of course to enjoy some live music and every type of apple dessert you could think of. Jasmine could think of a fair few. She hoped Ellie had some ideas for decorating the front windows of the clinic because she absolutely did not.

Jasmine Cline arrived at Benton a few minutes early. Clyde, their male Great Pyrenees Mountain Dog greeted her in the drive. He was nearly tall enough to put his head through her open window. When she opened the door he slurped her face hello.

"Hi Clyde, how's it going, boy?" Jasmine patted the gentle giant's head.

Clyde panted happily in response. Jasmine grabbed her coveralls and slipped them over her clothes, just in case. Great Pyrenees were notorious for ample shedding, and who knew what messes she would come across in the barn. She decided work boots wouldn't be necessary.

"Dr. Cline!" Sarah Benton called from the front porch. "Come on inside!" Jasmine and Clyde followed Sarah inside and into the big farm style kitchen where they joined Sarah's husband Chris and another Great Pyrenees, Greta.

"Hi, Dr. Cline, nice to see you again," Chris said warmly.

“Jasmine, please. It’s great to see you both.” Jasmine answered with a smile. They’d all known each other for years, but still, they insisted on calling her Doctor Cline.

Sarah poured two cups of coffee and passed one to Jasmine.

“So, I know you don’t work with the horses as much, but we’re very worried about Apollonia. I -- “Sarah began, sitting at the kitchen table.

“I already called Eric Canton, he should be here shortly.” Jasmine interrupted.

“Oh good!” Sarah breathed, visibly relieved. “I should have called him but you were already scheduled to come to see the dogs and I guess I was just panicked last night when I called your office. Sorry!”

“It’s okay; Eric and I work together often.” Jasmine smiled. Clyde barked and both dogs stood up. “That’ll be him, now.” Chris got up and went out to the porch. The men were chatting amicably as they returned.

“Jazz was just telling us you two work together often,” Chris mentioned to Eric.

A wide grin spread across Eric’s face. “That we do,” Eric answered. Though he was speaking to them all, he seemed to only have eyes for Jasmine.

Jasmine smiled, too, but shifted uncomfortably under his gaze. She set her coffee cup down and cleared her throat. “I suppose we should get to work now, too.”

Eric answered, “Yes, yes I suppose we should. Nice coveralls.” Eric grinned and Jazz tried not to blush.

The men went out to the stables to check on the Appaloosa mare. Eric seemed confident that she was just fine. Jasmine and Sarah stayed on the back porch where Jazz could give the big dogs a checkup.

"I wish you'd bring them in some time, I'd love to get them on the scales." Jasmine coaxed Clyde's mouth open so she could peek at his teeth.

"Oh, I know. I will. It's hard to travel with them. But I guess if we can haul around horses we could get the dogs into town, huh?" Sarah chuckled.

"Definitely." Of course, it was good to monitor the dogs' weight, but in this case, she was mostly curious. Great Pyrenees were one of the giant breeds, related to Great Danes, Newfoundlands, and St. Bernhards. They could get up to 160 pounds, and Clyde was one of the larger Great Pyres she had ever seen.

He was also a great big teddy bear. Jasmine often had more of a struggle examining Chihuahuas. Clyde lifted his paws so she could look at them, and sat calmly while she checked his pulse and watched his breathing. She repeated her exam with Greta, who was equally compliant and liked to lick.

"They're quite healthy. If you're planning to breed, I think they'll do fine." Jasmine said and started making some notes in the Benton's file.

"I think we may. Clyde is the last one of his line and I think Chris wants to keep the family going." Sarah patted the dog as she spoke.

"Well, good, then I'll have an excuse to get you into the office and weigh them. It'll be good to track Greta's weight during pregnancy. Keep me posted?" Jasmine asked brightly.

"Oh, I will. Puppies! I can't wait." Sarah chimed. "Should we go check on the boys?" Jasmine nodded and the pair walked through a vibrantly orange pumpkin patch and across the lawn, scattered with golden leaves down to the old stable. The building was clearly a relic of days past, maybe 100 years old, but immaculately kept. Jasmine loved this old farm. She and Sarah walked by rows of beautiful dappled Appaloosas to find the men standing in the last stall with a very pregnant Apollonia.

Eric had his face pressed to the huge mare's cheek, whispering to her. Eric was tall and lean, fit from hours and years working hard in barns just like this one. Jasmine couldn't help but notice how muscular his arms were, stretched up to stroke and soothe Apollonia. Since the top few buttons of his fitted shirt were undone, she could see the muscle of his chest heaving, too. Her eyes wandered to his face, strong jaw, full lips, his features baked golden from the sun. His hair had fallen forward, partially obscuring his eyes, but Jazz knew they were a deep stormy blue. While she watched him coax the horse to relax, she realized she was smiling. Eric was focused on the horse, but perhaps he noticed her watching him, those baby blues flicked up to meet hers and he smiled.

"I think she's going to be just fine," Eric spoke loudly enough for all three of them to hear. He brushed his hair back and stepped out of the box and shut it behind him. "She has some signs of placentitis, but I've given her a large dose of antibiotics. I do think I'd better keep a close eye on her, though, she's going to foal very soon."

"I thought she wasn't due until November? That's almost a month early." Sarah's concern was obvious in her voice.

"Well, I have it noted in her file that 340 days would be October 15th. So it's only a little more than a week early. It may take her a few days to get moving anyhow. And I'll be here to make sure everything goes smoothly. Okay?" Eric soothed Sarah's worries almost as easily as he had calmed the massive mare.

Sarah smiled, "Okay. Oh, I'm so glad you're here. I know I should be used to all this but I just panic if…."Sarah trailed off, seeming to reel herself in. "Thanks, Eric."

"My pleasure. I'll stop in here again this evening and you'll just see a lot of me until we've got a foal running around, is that alright with you two?" Eric asked.

"Of course, you'll be quite welcome. We'll make up the bed in the room over the garage in case you decide to stay. I'm sure Chris will be around if you need help at all, and Ben should be home tomorrow. He's going to help out with the Festival Fair. " Benjamin Collins was Sarah's younger brother. Naturally, the Appaloosas would be featured at the fair, and Jasmine was quite sure the Bentons played a substantial role in the pumpkin patch events as well.

"Come get me if you need anything at all." Chris smiled and they all started toward the farmhouse.

Jasmine and Eric trailed behind. "Call me, too, if you need an extra hand." Jasmine offered.

"Can I call if I don't need help?" Eric quipped. Jazz looked up at him and realized he was teasing.

"Maybe just send me a text." She laughed and caught up with the others.

CHAPTER TWO

When Jasmine got back to the office it was a stark contrast to the silence she'd experienced that morning. Dogs and cats and their families lined the lobby seats, Ellie seemed to be visiting with a large scarlet Macaw, and their vet techs were hustling pets in and out of exam rooms. Jasmine didn't envy Claire, who must have seen a dozen patients already this morning. She poked her head into Claire's office.

"Oh, I'm so happy to see you!" Claire exclaimed. She looked a little worse for wear, her white coat had various kinds of fur all over it and her bright red hair, usually pulled back nearly, was tousled all over out of its ponytail. "What a morning!"

"I thought you might be hungry," Jazz said, plopping down a brown bag from Colby's Deli. "What on earth is happening out there?"

"Walk-ins! All the walk-ins! I guess everyone got their vaccination reminders at the same time, and no one thought to make an appointment." Claire pulled a sandwich out of the bag and dug in.

"Well let me just get out of these coveralls and I'll take over for a while." Jasmine grabbed her sandwich, which she knew she wouldn't get to eat for some time.

The afternoon was a blur of quick check-ups and shots. Jasmine worked closely with their newest tech, Brian, who was studying for Veterinary school. He was a huge help, and while they were very busy, they made it to 4:30 without any major catastrophes. Everyone was seen and treated, and the lobby emptied. Jasmine sat down to update everyone's files online and maybe eat that sandwich. She had just started the first patient's notes when she overheard Ellie in the lobby, explaining to someone that the clinic would be closed soon. She offered to make them an appointment. Jasmine sighed and glanced longingly at her sandwich, still wrapped. She got up and went to the front desk.

At the front desk stood a woman straight out of a classic Hollywood film. She had on a pale rose gown, gathered at her waist. Her blonde hair was brushed to the side in waves and neatly curled. Even her makeup looked like something from another time.

"Hi, I'm Jasmine Cline. It's okay Ellie; I can make time for one more." Jasmine stepped forward and extended her hand. The starlet shook it delicately.

"Oh thank you, thank you. I'm Lily Day." Her voice was soft and sweet, maybe too well practiced. She bent to lift a pet carrier and set it on the counter. A small white Shih Tzu peered out at them, sneezing repeatedly. "This is my Daisy. She's been having these seizures all morning." Lily sniffled. "I didn't know, because I was in rehearsals. I would have brought her in sooner but…" she trailed off.

"Well let's take a look. Brian?" Jasmine called into the back of the clinic. He popped his head out of exam room 2. "Hey will you bring my new friend Daisy to exam 2 for me?" Jasmine went to grab a few things from her medkit.

When Jasmine got to the exam room, little Daisy was standing on the table, still sneezing. Brian was holding her gently in place and Lily was pacing on kitten heels behind the table, hands around on her hips.

"Don't panic, Miss Day. I don't think Daisy is having a seizure." Jasmine mentioned, running her hands along the little dog.

"Oh, it's Mrs. Day," Lily corrected. "You don't?" She stepped up next to Brian.

"No, I don't. I think she's reverse sneezing. It's really common in flat-faced breeds, like Shih Tzus, Pugs, Pekingese and so on." Jasmine clicked on a large overhead light and tipped the dog's face up to examine her nose. She picked up a pair of rubber-tipped tweezers. "And…." She grasped something in Daisy's nose and started to pull. "Often triggered by an allergen or something caught in their nose." Jasmine tugged and revealed a small blade of grass that had been stuck in the poor dog's snout.

Jasmine started to stroke the dog's neck and face and the sneezing subsided. Lily sighed audibly.

"Oh, how can I ever thank you? I thought she was done for, for sure." Lily definitely had a flair for drama.

"You see how I'm petting her here? If this happens again, rub her neck and chest like so." Jasmine demonstrated. "I'll give you some mild antihistamines, give her one tonight. She'll sleep well, and she could probably use the rest after today."

"Oh, I could too!" Lily laughed. "But I won't get much tonight."

"Yes, you said you were rehearsing. You have a show?" Jasmine handed Daisy over to Brian and made some notes.

"Yes, our full dress rehearsal is tonight and we open tomorrow night. Musical Comedy of Murders. Have you heard of it?" Jasmine shook her head. "Well, it's a comedy whodunit set in the 40s. I play Nikki Crandall. My husband Sam is in it, too, he plays Michael Kelly. OH! Sam! I've got to call him and let him know Daisy is okay, he'll be worried sick!" Lily whisked out of the room, cell phone in hand.

"Well, at least that explains the outfit. She's a trip, huh? It's like talking to Marilyn Monroe." Brain wondered aloud.

"I guess she takes her acting seriously." Jasmine shrugged. "Take Daisy out to the lobby and then fill this script, will you?" She passed him a slip of paper and went back to her office.

Jasmine had just unwrapped that sandwich when the door to her office flew open. Lily Day appeared and rushed over to the desk. She grabbed Jasmine in an awkward but genuine hug.

“I really just can’t ever thank you enough! I was so worried about my Daisy! Thank you, Dr. Cline! Thank you! I’ll leave some tickets to the show for you at the box, okay?” Lily smiled sweetly and stepped back into the doorway.

“Oh thank you, it’s no trouble. I appreciate that. I -” Lily sneezed so hard Jasmine couldn’t continue. “I -” Lily sneezed again, harder. She stepped toward the desk, sneezing again and again.

“Mrs. Day, are you alright? Reverse sneezing isn’t contagious.” Jasmine joked but was genuinely concerned for the actress.

“Um. I’m alright. Do you work with horses, Dr. Cline?” Lily sniffed and shook her head as if she were trying to clear it.

“Sometimes, I saw a horse this morning,” Jasmine answered, quite puzzled.

“That’s it, then. I’m deathly allergic to horses! I love them too, but I just can’t be near them. Even a little whiff of their hair… I’ll need some Benadryl to make it through the night, but I’ll be okay. Man, if I touch one, look out!” Lily stood up and composed herself. She smoothed her dress and her perfect curls.

“Oh I’m sorry; it must be from my coveralls I was wearing, they’re in that bag hanging on the door.” Jasmine nodded to the gym bag, hanging in its usual place beside her mirror.

“It’s okay - I’ll be fine. I had better get going though. Thanks again, Dr. Cline, you’re a treasure. Lily smiled and hurried out.

Jasmine sat down and finally bit into her sandwich. She made some quick notes in Daisy's file "no horses, owner allergy." She leaned back, running her conversation with the actress over in her mind. She felt terrible about triggering Lily's allergies, and she remembered the tickets to see the show. Jasmine wondered; who on earth would she take to see a play? Merritt Valley was home to The Lyric, an historic theatre that boasted past performances by vaudeville greats like Mae West and W.C. Fields. In recent times it housed several local theater groups and Merritt Valley High School often performed plays and concerts there as well. Jasmine enjoyed the theater but hadn't been in some time. She guessed she could ask Claire to go watch Lily, her husband and the others perform. Then the image of Eric Canton in a suit, standing in the gilded auditorium briefly played in her mind. She ran a finger over her lips. Now, that was quite an idea.

CHAPTER THREE

Thursday morning rolled around and Jasmine Cline got dressed with a little more care than usual. She told herself it was not because she planned to stop to check on Eric and the Benton's mare, Apollonia. She just wanted to look nice for herself. Of course, she had to dress for a farm in autumn, so she slide into her favorite form-fitting jeans and tucked her tank top into them before zipping up. She slid a buttery soft flannel in brown and cream tones and buttoned it up before sliding her feet into knee high riding boots. She tugged their zippers in place over her jeans and stood up. The earthy colors of her flannel played nicely with her deep bronze skin.

She ran three small French braids into the top of her hair and smoothed the rest of it into a high pony. A few curls tried to escape and she tamed them into place with a bit of pomade and fine bristle brush. She ran some mascara over her long naturally curled lashes and slid some sultry brown lipstick over her lush pout. She stepped back and gave herself a look. Not too bad at all, she thought and grabbed her bag and keys.

Grand Avenue was bustling with activity this morning. Men were hanging the Festival of Leaves sign over the street, and a couple of blocks down, another group of people was changing the marquee for The Lyric Theatre. "Musical Comedy of Murders," stood in big black letters. People had gathered in front of the clothing boutique Blackbird, where they were setting up their fall decor. Of course, the local bakery and deli The Muffin Man hummed with people buzzing in and out with bags of pastries and hot cups of coffee.

Jazz decided to get a coffee herself but hoped she could talk herself out of a pastry. The shop smelled like all the best parts of fall, baked apples and cinnamon wafting out from the kitchen.

"Mornin Jazz! Can I talk you into a caramel apple puff?" one of the servers, Jack called out from behind the counter.

"No, no, not today Jack! I've got to save my junk food points for the festival."

"You sure? The sign's going up, technically the festival starts today!" Jack grinned over the display case, filled with all manner of divine treats, mostly apple and pumpkin this time of year.

"Oh, Jack. Fine. Give me half a dozen; I'll feed the whole office." Jasmine gave a dramatic eye roll and pretended to be annoyed.

"You got it! Sweets are sweeter, shared!" Jack made quick work of boxing up the pastries while Jasmine ordered her coffee. She paid for breakfast, dropped a tip in the jar, and slipped outside. The weather had cooled since yesterday, the air was deliciously chilled. She balanced the steaming travel cup with her treats and work bag for half a block between Merritt Valley Mobile Veterinary Clinic and the deli. Ellie saw her through the window and grabbed the door.

"Morning Boss! What have you got there?" Ellie was her usual bright self this morning.

"I may have brought some caramel apple puffs," Jasmine responded and set the box down on the counter. She slide one of the treats out for herself and headed back to her office. "Let the others know, will you?" Ellie nodded. "Hey El, do you think you can manage the Window display for the Festival this year? You've got such a knack for it."

"Really? I'd love to!" Ellie replied.

"Great. Use the business credit card and get whatever you need, there should be a line item for it in this year's budget." The Festival was a big deal around town, if they didn't participate, people would notice. Jasmine was relieved to have Ellie handle this; she took her pastry and headed back to her office.

"Okay, Boss!" Ellie chimed, joyfully.

"Quit callin me Boss!" Jasmine called over her shoulder, chuckling. She could hear Ellie's laughter as she shut her office door. She had a busy day ahead. She enjoyed the pastry over files for today's patients. Checked her messages and returned a few calls. She started to see patients at 9 am. Before she had a chance to sit down, it was already two pm. Jasmine pulled out her cell and sent Claire a text. "What's for lunch?" Claire answered by wandering in and sitting down.

"What have we gotten ourselves into?" She asked, only half joking.

"Goodness, I don't know. Let's run away to Barbados." both women laughed.

"Lunch huh? Should I call for Chinese?" Claire asked

"Sounds great," Jasmine answered and took a breath. She wasn't sure how to broach the subject and opted to simply blurt her question out. "You think it's okay to ask a man out?"

Claire looked up from her phone, her eyebrows raised in surprise. She licked her lips and considered that for a moment. "Well it's 2020, of course, you can ask a man out. Did you have someone in mind, or are you just taking volunteers from the street?" she joked.

"Oh, you know who." Jasmine quipped back.

Claire sighed and smiled. "The Horse Whisperer. Eric? You're finally going to ask him out?"

"Well, I think if I wait for him we'll be old and grey before we sit down to dinner together." Jazz responded.

"I think you're right about that. Jazz, of course you can ask that man out. And now I see why you're all cuted up today." Claire smiled and picked her phone back up.

“I am not cuted up. I look like this every day.” Jasmine joked.

“Uh-huh. Nice lipstick.” Claire winked and ordered their lunch.

It was nearly four pm when Jasmine caught sight of her office chair again. She realized she had been stalling. Her last patient had already checked out and was probably home by now. She’d stocked some supplies and chatted with all the staff. She had even changed a light bulb in the hall.

In the years they’d worked together, Eric Canton had given her no reason to be so nervous about going to keep him company in a stable. Still, she couldn’t stop herself from procrastinating. She decided to make a large thermos of coffee. She fiddled around on her phone, deleting old messages, checking social media. Finally, she stood up. Girl, you’re being plain ridiculous, she thought. She checked her hair and freshened her lipstick before grabbing her things. Okay, Jasmine, she thought, time to GO.

CHAPTER FOUR

Jasmine arrived at the Benton Ranch just before five pm. She pulled up and parked next to Eric's truck and hopped out with her thermos. There were several other cars parked in the drive, and she could hear lots of conversation and laughter coming from the old farmhouse. Jasmine thought she would leave the Bentons to their family dinner uninterrupted, deciding to go straight to the stable instead. Leaves crunched beneath her boots as she made her way and Greta let out a soft ruff of acknowledgment as she passed the back porch. Red maple leaves reflected the orange of an autumn sunset as the breeze gave a warning of cooler nights on the horizon.

Eric Canton was propped up on a bench at the end of the stables; his long legs stretched the length of it, with papers all over his lap and a tablet in his hands. He was lost in whatever project he was working on, but a huge smile spread over his face when he noticed Jasmine approaching.

"Now that's a pleasant surprise." Eric slid over and set his legs on the ground. He collected his papers and tablet, gesturing for Jasmine to sit.

"I couldn't let you have all the fun." Jasmine smiled and sat down. Eric was dressed for sitting in a barn all night. A grey flannel button-up shirt and warm fleece vest, dark denim, and heavy boots. Jasmine glanced over at Apolonia's stall but couldn't see the mare. "How's she doing?"

"She's just starting to get colicky. I think we'll have a foal before the night is out." Eric answered. Jasmine knew him well enough to know he was confident that Apollonia and her foal would be fine. She had seen him concerned for a patient before, and she'd seen him feign nonchalance for farmers when he was. There was no pretense about him now. He brushed his hair back from his face and just looked at her for a moment. She felt her cheeks flush. Eric chuckled under his breath.

“How are things at the new clinic?” Eric asked and sat back. Apollonia shifted behind her, snorting and grunting uncomfortably. Eric nodded at Jasmine to carry on.

“Oh… awesome. And exhausting. I don’t think either Claire or I realized the level of demand in town. I’m starting to think there must be 3 pets for every person in Merritt. Some days we’re more than double booked. And the walk-ins. I don’t know, we might have to rethink that policy. Most days we don’t have a chance to sit down!” Jasmine realized she was rambling and stopped herself.

“I seem to remember mentioning the high demand for veterinary care around here.” Eric teased. “I can’t tell you how many cats and poodles I saw before you two moved home. I’m sure things will level off in time. It hasn’t been a year yet, and lots of people just did without before you opened.”

“I hope you’re right. Of course, so much business is good but I don’t want us to burn ourselves out. Getting involved with the tech program has been so helpful. Thank you, for suggesting that.” She squeezed his forearm. Before they’d opened the clinic last winter, he mentioned that the community college vet. tech program always needed positions for students to complete clinicals. He had even helped her navigate all the paperwork and steps to get their clinic approved for the program.

“No sweat.” He smiled. From her stall, Apollonia whinnied and seemed to turn in a full circle. The mare was getting restless, which was normal at this stage.

“How’s your business been?” Jasmine swallowed her nerves. That was not the question she wanted to ask him.

“Steady. More people are getting into cattle so that’s been good news for me. Vaccinations, immunizations, calving, they keep me busy. And cast - “he coughed, “Uh. Castrations.” He looked down suddenly fascinated with his own hands. “Sorry, I… didn’t mean to.” Eric trailed off and laughed awkwardly.

Was it possible Eric Canton was nervous, too? If this is what Eric looked like when he blushed, Jasmine was tempted to make that happen more often. She laughed with him.

"It's really okay, Eric. You remember I'm a vet, too, right? You know I spay and neuter a few dozen patients a week." She smiled at him and he seemed to relax. Apollonia

"Hey, how's your mom?" he asked.

"Good. She's been canning and freezing things all week. I don't know how one woman manages such a big garden. She keeps bringing me huge baskets of tomatoes and cucumbers. She just loves having me so close again."

"I can relate." Eric's eyes said he wasn't teasing this time. Jasmine smiled and his face lit up with that great big genuine smile of his. Jasmine swallowed and took a breath.

"So, I met Lily Day yesterday." she started.

"Did you? Uh. Who is Lily Day?" Eric asked.

"She's an actress straight out of an old Hollywood movie. Her Shih Tzu had snorted a piece of grass." Jasmine could feel her speech speeding up.

"Aw, poor pup. Did you fix him up?"

"Oh, yeah. She's just fine." Jazz corrected, gently. "Lily was so delighted she gave me tickets to the play. It opens tomorrow night." Jasmine suddenly lost her ability to speak.

"Yeah? What play?" Eric implored.

"Um. Music Murder Mystery Something or Other?" The name of the show completely eluded her and they shared a laugh. "Anyhow, I have two tickets. You want to see it with me?" Whew. She managed to spit it out. Jasmine had never been so frustrated by her own tongue.

"I'd love to," Eric answered without hesitation.

"Great. I think it will be fun."

"Oh, it will." Eric smiled again. "I'll pick you up? Around six?"

"Perfect." Jasmine couldn't stop smiling, herself. "You're not going to sleep in the barn, are you?" The mare in the stall behind her could not be ignored. She was snorting and bellowing, stamping her feet and flipping her tail.

"You think she'd let me sleep? Na, I don't think that will be necessary." Before Jazz could answer, Apollonia made a big fuss and flopped down in the straw in her stall. Eric stood up and peered over the edge.

"Is she alright?" Jasmine inquired.

He nodded. "Yeah, she'll get up and lay down a few times before the big show. I think I'll be in bed before midnight at this rate. I should check on her, though." He glanced at Jasmine.

"Well, I'll leave you to it. This coffee is for you," she said and set the thermos down on the bench.

"Oh thank you, I may need some of that before the night is out. Tomorrow at six? Eric reached for the latch to the horse stall.

"Tomorrow at six," Jasmine repeated wistfully and turned to head out of the ancient stable house.

The sun had set, and the October breeze had a bit of bite to it now. Jasmine made quick work of the walk through the pumpkin patch and up to the Benton's back door. She tapped hard enough to be heard over the conversation in the kitchen. Sarah Benton opened the door with a smile.

"Oh, Dr. Cline! Come on inside!" Sarah stepped aside, revealing a room full of happy, well-fed people. The remnants of an old fashioned feast lay spread on the table, and two pies seemed to be missing several pieces each. One apple and one pumpkin, if Jasmine wasn't mistaken. "Are you hungry? The boys have made a mess but there's plenty if I can interest you in a plate?" Sarah gestured for Jasmine to take a seat at the table.

"Oh, no, no I'm fine." She sat down as one of Sarah's brothers pulled out the seat for her. "But, I might be talked into a piece of that pie." Jasmine grinned. Two treats in one day. She may need to go for an extra long run tomorrow, but she felt no shame. She thought the best baked treats arrived in autumn.

"You just have to!" Chris passed her a small plate. "Pumpkin or apple?"

"Apple, please."

"An excellent choice, miss. My favorite." He grinned and sliced her a piece.

Sarah made introductions while Jasmine dug into her piece of pie. Jasmine had met most of the boys and their wives or girlfriends, just around town, and Chris's little sister Angelica had brought her Great Pyrenees for a checkup last year when Jasmine still worked for Lee Hwan in Queen City. They all said their hellos and caught up over pie and coffee. Jasmine felt so at home here, for a moment she wondered what it might be like to live on a farm like this one. A house big enough to host all your favorite people, home-cooked food, big dogs snoring around and under the table.

Sarah interrupted her daydream. "Hey, how's Apollonia? These boys are supposed to be her to help if she needs to be lifted or turned." Sarah's scolding was playful, but the men did stand up and start pulling on jackets and sweaters.

“Well she’s pretty irritated but Eric said she’s doing great,” Jasmine answered, watching the troop prepare to go out. “She had just laid down when I came up here.”

The guys all said their farewells and headed out into the night. Jasmine decided she had probably get going, too.

“I’m glad you’ve got so much help. You can call me if you need anything, but I’m sure you won’t. Apollonia is in great hands.” Jazz stood up and moved toward the kitchen door.

Sarah smiled and opened the door for her. “Somehow, I don’t think you’re talking about our brothers. Maybe a certain beefcake doctor?” She grinned devilishly.

“Maybe.” Jasmine laughed. She felt herself flush and Sarah hugged her.

“You’re right, about those hands,” Sarah whispered. Something about the way she said that reassured Jasmine. The hug also reminded her she needed to make more time for her friends. After all, that was, in part, why she’d moved back to Merritt. A smaller town meant more time for friends and family. Time to build a life. Perhaps time for a relationship, too.

Jasmine headed out into the night. It was so crisp out; a little condensation had formed on the Jeep’s windshield. She flicked on the heat and defrost and sat back in her seat. As she waited for the view to clear, she went over her conversation with Eric. Had she been too awkward? No. He seemed just as excited as she was. A date! She couldn’t remember the last time she had gone on a date. Her stomach fluttered again. She shook her head, laughing at herself and buckled up.

Friday morning, Jasmine heard Stevie Wonder crooning, “For Once in my Life,” and opened her eyes. She rolled over and picked up her phone to turn up the music. As she started to hit the volume button she saw a new message had arrived just after one am. Who would have texted her at that hour? She flipped it open to reveal a picture of a beautifully dappled black and white spotted foal. He was standing in front of his mother, Apollonia, already back on her feet. He looked like he was smiling.

"Meet Apollo. He arrived about midnight, right on schedule. See you tonight." Eric had captioned the photo.

Jasmine grinned and cranked up her upbeat Motown morning playlist. She hit a couple of smiley faces and, "Nice work, mister - see you tonight!" Send. She stretched and climbed out of bed. She tugged her sheets and blanket back into place and tossed the decorative pillows onto the bed. She danced a little to the music while she picked out her outfit and got ready for her shower. It was going to be a good day.

The sidewalks of Andrews Avenue were lined with straw bales, pumpkins, and scarecrows. People dressed in their cozy October gear were adding finishing touches to their Festival of Leaves decorations and gabbing over hot travel mugs, mostly from the local shop. Jasmine did not doubt that a few of those cups contained pumpkin spice flavored beverages.

"Morning Ellie!" Jasmine chimed before Ellie had a chance to.

"Wow, morning boss! You're in a good mood this morning." Ellie was stacking charts, no doubt preparing for the day.

"That I am. Any messages for me this morning?"

"Just a cancellation - Paul something or other won't be able to make his 2 o'clock. He said he'll call back and reschedule." Ellie passed the stack of files over.

"Oh, good. Maybe I can sneak out early." Jazz winked and headed to her office.

It looked like a typical Friday at the office. Jasmine saw two parrots in the morning. Lucy, a vibrant green Amazon parrot was her first appointment of the day. Lucy's owner, Mark, was excited about the Festival of Leaves and chattered pleasantly about his plans to attend the parade, and take his daughter to the pumpkin patch. Jasmine coaxed Lucy onto the digital scale and wrote down her weight before she set her back on her perch.

"I think they have hayrides this year, too. You should check it out if you have time." Mark mentioned.

"Oh, I'll see if I can work that in." Jasmine evaluated Lucy's eyes, ears, nares, and beak. She made a few notes and ran her finger over the bird's belly. Lucy sang a happy little tune as Jazz examined her plumage and vent, spine, and finally her legs and feet. She checked some things off the list in Lucy's chart.

"Did you bring samples?" Jazz inquired.

"Oh, yes, fun stuff," Mark answered and produced a Ziploc baggie with a small plastic container inside. Fecal samples.

"Thanks, Mark. We'll run some diagnostics for parasites and such, but Lucy seems to be in great health. You trim her wings and nails yourself?" Jasmine took off her gloves and tossed them.

"Yeah I do, Lucy is my third parrot, and I've picked up a lot along the way." Mark extended his arm and Lucy hopped on. She transferred into her travel cage without a fuss.

"Well, you're doing a great job. Most people bring their birds in to get their wings done. I've got to go see an African Grey about that next. Take care and maybe I'll see you at the hayride." Mark smiled and waved as Jasmine left the exam room.

Jasmine passed a veterinary intern, Brian in the hall.

"Someone's waiting for you in exam 4." He mentioned as they met.

"Thanks. There's a sample in one, can you see that it gets to the lab?"

"Sure!" Brian replied over his shoulder.

Jasmine found Irene Hudson and her African Grey waiting in Exam room 4. The large grey and white parrot was aptly named Doctor Grey and affectionately referred to as Doc. He was a favorite of the entire staff, who saw him every 6 to 8 weeks when he needed his nails clipped. Doc fluffed his feathers slightly as Jasmine entered the room but immediately settled back down.

"Hi, Doc," Jasmine said, brightly.

"Hi Doc." the bird responded. Jasmine didn't know how much Doc understood, but she certainly enjoyed their conversations. She opened a cabinet and got out a nail trimming perch, which she attached to the exam table. Normally she would ask the pet owner to move their bird, but Irene knew the drill. She took Doctor Grey out of his cage and set him on the perch. He stretched his wings and imitated a phone ring.

Jasmine raised a brow. "That's new." She pulled out her nail trimmers from a nearby drawer.

"Mhm." Irene nodded. "I thought it was fun until he started to do it all the time. I'm missing calls because I think it's just Doc playing!"

Jasmine got close to Doc to let him get used to her. When he lowered his head and half closed his eyes, she scritched his head gently. After a few moments she started to trim his nails and he didn't put up a fight.

"Hmm. There are a few ways you could get him to stop ringing. I would try sitting him down for 10 or 15 minutes a day. Bring a handful of treats and teach him a new sound. Preferably a sound you like more than a ringing phone.

"I would also change your ringtone. You know how to do that?"

Irene nodded, "I keep meaning to."

“Okay, so I suggest you do that. I’m sure Ellie at the front desk would be happy to help you, too. The last thing I’d offer is that you totally ignore him when he rings. Don’t scold him, don’t even make eye contact. If you combine that with teaching him something new, with any luck he’ll stop pretending to be a phone.” As Jasmine finished, Doc rang right on cue. Both women laughed.

Jasmine buzzed through her other appointments and even worked through lunch. Since her last two appointments were canceled, she decided to take the afternoon off. She would grab some lunch then, and find something to wear for the play tonight.

Around two pm she popped her head into Claire’s office.

“Hey, my last couple of appointments were canceled. You need me for anything?”

“No, I think I can hold down the fort. Where you off to?” Claire asked over a pile of microwave noodles.

“I’ve got to go find something to wear to the show tonight.”

“Oh, yes, the play. Did you ask our handsome colleague after all?” Claire smiled.

“I was a ball of nerves but I did manage to ask, yes. It’s been so long since I had a reason to dress up; I think I need something new.” Jasmine replied.

“A new dress or outfit for a date is a good idea.” Claire grinned. “Try not to be so nervous. You know Eric. He’s an old friend. Think of him that way and quit stressing out.”

“I’ll try.” Jasmine turned to walk away.

“And send me a picture of the outfit!” Claire called behind her.

Jasmine stepped out the front door of Merritt Valley Mobile Veterinary Clinic. The scent of straw and fallen leaves drifted around her and the subtle October sun fell over her face. She took a deep breath, savoring the scent. She slipped on her sunglasses and wandered down toward Blackbird. Lily Day was coming out of the shop when she reached it.

Again, Mrs. Day was dressed like a 40's movie star. A long black a-line skirt with what seemed to be endless teal ruffles peeking from underneath. A matching teal blouse was tucked into the skirt, her narrow waist accentuated with a large belt. A wide-brimmed hat covered her blonde curls. She couldn't have blended in if she wanted to. Jasmine suspected blending in was never Lily's goal.

"Oh, Doctor Cline!" Lily lifted the backs of her fingers to her lips in a gesture of surprise.

"Jasmine, please. Hello Lily, find anything good in there?"

"Too many things! I think Sam might kill me when he sees the credit card bill." The young actress giggled. "Are you coming to the show tonight? Please say you'll be there!"

"I'll be there, let's hope I can find a dress inside." Jasmine nodded toward the boutique.

"Oh, I'm sure you will! Come and see me after? I'd love for Sam to meet you." Lily slid on some huge sunglasses.

"I'd love to." Jasmine answered."

"Wonderful! I'd better go, see you tonight!" Lily swirled off, a flurry of shopping bags and skirt.

"Break a leg!" Jazz called behind her. She turned and entered the shop.

Blackbird was a quirky little boutique brightly decorated with hints of Parisian design. Unique garments for women of all sizes lined the racks and displays. Everything at Blackbird had been expertly chosen by Moira, the shop's owner. She was a full-figured beauty, not much older than Jasmine. She always had edgy haircuts, sometimes with pops of bright colors, and dressed like a classy rock star. Today Moira was wearing all black, leather pants and had a vibrant purple scarf tied around her neck. A hint of that same purple peeked out under her otherwise black hair.

"Jazz! It's great to see you! Been a while." Moira called from behind the front counter. She came around and gave Jasmine a squeeze.

"It really has. I don't have much use for fashion lately; I'm forever covered in fur and feathers." Jasmine chuckled.

"I bet you are! What are you looking for today?"

"Well, you know that woman who just left? Lily?" Jasmine inquired.

"Oh yeah, she's in here all the time. I just did a custom order for her. That's what she was picking up. Well, part of it, anyhow! She's practically keeping me in business." Moira laughed.

"Looked like it. Can I ask what she ordered?" she whispered. Jasmine was a little fascinated by the small-town star.

"Sure, it's no secret. Well, you've seen her style. Like an old time starlet? She wanted a dressing gown. A big full one with embroidery and the fur around the sleeves and all. It was harder to find than I expected." Moira picked up a wholesaler's catalog off the counter and flipped to a page marked with a neon yellow post it. She tipped the book toward Jasmine, revealing a beautiful robe, the likes of which Jasmine had never seen off-screen. The page was full of similar robes and matching nightdresses.

"Wow. Those are gorgeous. I've never seen one in real life."

“Neither had I to be honest. She got the matching gown, too.” Moira flopped the heavy book back down on her counter. “What does Lily have to do with your shopping?”

“Well, I’m going to see her play tonight. I have a date… a first date. So I…” Jasmine trailed off.

“So you want to look like a million bucks.” Moira finished for her.

“Exactly. Can you help me?” Jasmine pleaded.

“Can I help you? Babe, when I’m through with you, you’ll look so good your date might just propose.” She laughed again. “C’mon, you’re an eight, right? I’ve got some dresses that will look divine on you.” Moira slipped through the racks swooping up dresses along the way. They arrived at the changing rooms with a pile of dresses for Jasmine to try on.

Usually, Jasmine would have just chosen something in her size and called it good. Today she enjoyed trying on the different looks, though a few of them were too outrageous to consider. There was no way she was going to the theatre in a silver lame or zebra print dress. Still, she and Moira got a good laugh out of them when she modeled them.

She finally settled on a gorgeous indigo dress that wrapped snugly around her waist, flared at the hips, and came down to a pencil skirt just below the knee. She and Moira decided the color flattered her deep bronze skin and the shape accentuated her curves while maintaining enough mystery to be classy. It was sort of perfect.

It was just about four pm when Jasmine slipped out of Blackbird arms loaded with bags. Moira may have talked her into a few other outfits, perfect for autumn. She stashed her bags in the passenger seat of the Jeep and headed home. She would have plenty of time to unwind and do some pre-date pampering.

Jasmine rolled up to her modest little house on Hattrick Avenue. It was a peaceful neighborhood, mostly singles and retired couples. Her house had a cottage look outside; short square hedges lined the stone walk up to the front deck. Flower beds and decorative trees grew just in front of the deck; of course, all the flowers were gone this time of year. Her apple tree was doing nicely; she grabbed an apple on her way inside.

The inside of Jasmine's house was more modern. She had the place repainted before she moved in, and had the old 90's carpeting replaced with antique white wood planks. She had the sinks and fixtures all updated as well, and of course, she'd brought all her furniture from her apartment in the city. Clean lines in complementary neutral tones with pops of white and a few muted colors. Jasmine's mom hated the juxtaposition between the home's old-fashioned fairy tale exterior and the clean contemporary interior design. Jasmine, however, loved it. It made her feel at home and she knew it would increase her resale value.

Jasmine plopped down her armload of shopping bags on the couch. She flipped on the TV for background noise. Some talk show ladies were demonstrating a method of cupcake decorating which resulted in cupcakes that looked like caramel apples. Jasmine took her dress to her room and hung it up, then poked through her rather large shoe collection. When she found the perfect pair of T-strap kitten heels, she set them below the dress and stepped back to admire the look. She smiled and chose a small clutch to go with the ensemble. Something about this whole dating thing made her feel like she was getting ready for a school formal. Prom, or given the season, maybe homecoming. She chuckled at herself and ran a hot bath.

As she soaked in the scented bubbles she wondered about the evening. Would Eric treat her as he always had; a friend and colleague, but nothing more? Or would he get into the romance of the evening? Jasmine wondered if Eric could be romantic. She couldn't help daydreaming a little about their first kiss. Goodness. Would there be a kiss? What if they just shook hands and said goodnight?

Jasmine laughed out loud. She was being ridiculous.

After her bath, she made herself some tea and took the time to smooth her long dark ringlets with a straightening iron. She rarely bothered with that but thought a date called for something different. She took extra care with her makeup, full subtle eye shadow, and even highlighted her cheekbones with a soft shimmering powder. She filled in her brows a bit and tried out a new lipstick, a deep red. She dotted on a little cocoa-scented perfume and put on her favorite gold necklace. The delicate wishbone pendant lay just between her collarbones.

It was just about 5:45 pm by the time she was ready. More than ready, really. She had fussed with her already finished hair almost ten minutes before she decided to go sit in the living room and wait for Eric. She gave herself a final once over and left her room feeling like that million bucks Moira had promised.

Jasmine had hardly entered the living room when her doorbell rang. She glanced at the time on her cell. Huh. He's early. She thought this must be a good sign. She stopped for a moment before opening the door.

Eric Canton stood in her doorway, polished and gorgeous. He wore a dusky grey suit with a thin blue tie. He had traded in his work boots for black leather oxfords and he had smoothed his usually unruly blond waves back with a side part. He looked classic and at ease in his suit. Jasmine realized she was kind of, gaping at him. She felt herself flush.

Eric leaned in and kissed her cheek hello. "You look amazing. I'm sorry I'm early. I… I couldn't wait." He stepped back and smiled that big inviting smile of his.

"Oh, I don't mind at all," Jasmine responded honestly. "You look great, too. Really great." She grabbed her long autumn dress coat from the rack at the door and before she could slip it on, Eric stepped in and grabbed it, holding it open for her. She shrugged into its warmth.

"You ready?" He held the door open.

“All set,” she replied and they stepped outside. The air had turned cooler so quickly. The wind was cooler still and Jasmine was pleased she’d remembered her coat. Eric opened the passenger side door to his sedan and she slid inside. It was immaculately clean, she wondered if anyone had ever driven it before.

“Did you buy this today?” She teased him once he was behind the wheel. He laughed.

“No, no. It just doesn’t get out of the garage much.” Eric answered. Jasmine was pretty sure she’d only ever seen his pickup.

They made their way toward the heart of the small town they both called home. A little small talk about work, a few jokes between them, and Jasmine’s nerves were already gone. Though, the butterflies did swirl around in her stomach from time to time.

Eric pulled into the parking lot at Taste of Rome. The lot was nearly full. Jasmine guessed everyone in town must have had the same idea for a pre-show meal.

Eric spoke her thought out loud. “Everyone else must have the same plans, huh? I guess we could go to the diner, but I figured it wasn’t a burger and fries kind of night.”

“Agreed. It’s okay; everyone will see us together at the play, anyhow.” For a second Jasmine worried he might not want the whole town to know they were on a date.

“I’m counting on it.” He grinned. Her worries fell aside immediately. He turned off the engine and came around to open her door. He even put out a hand to help her up. Again, she was reminded of a school dance. Though, she didn’t remember finding any of the boys in high school as handsome as Eric looked tonight.

The crowd inside the charming Italian restaurant seemed to agree with her. Jasmine wasn't shy but she felt rather uncomfortable as people turned to check them out as they entered. She could feel the entire room stare as they were greeted by a cheerful hostess and lead through the tables to a quiet corner out of the way. As they sat she realized she could hardly see anyone else from here.

"I didn't even know they had private seating here." She murmured.

"I called earlier to see if they did. I didn't know it would be so crowded, but now I'm really glad I did." Eric said over his wine menu.

Jasmine was impressed. "Me, too."

A server ran over a list of specials. Rigatoni Arrabiata, Fusilli Con Pesto with chicken and Salmon cetriolini. Jasmine ordered the rigatoni; Eric ordered the salmon and the wine. The server returned quickly and poured two glasses. Jasmine swirled hers and gave it a sniff while Eric just dove in and took a sip. He nodded in approval and sat his glass down.

"So. Any idea what the play is about?" he asked.

"Um. Murder? And music?" she laughed and he joined her. "I have no idea to be honest."

"It doesn't matter, to be honest." Eric was still smiling but his tone and eyes told her he was serious. They held eye contact for a moment and Jasmine could nearly hear her heartbeat. His eyes shone a starlit blue in this light and the way he gazed at her tonight was captivating.

The food and wine were delicious though Jasmine hardly noticed. The conversation flowed easily and they laughed so much she thought she could probably skip crunches during her workout tomorrow. When the bill arrived Jasmine reached for it but Eric clicked his tongue and slipped it deftly out of her hands.

“Hey. I invited you, so it should be my treat.” She insisted.

“Nonsense. Besides, you scored us free tickets.” He slipped his credit card into the small folder and passed it to the server with a smile. Jasmine shook her head but she enjoyed the traditional gesture.

As they left the restaurant, Eric gently touched her back, almost guiding her through the crowded space. If people noticed them this time, Jasmine wasn’t concerned.

When the pair arrived at the Lyric Theatre, people had gathered in pairs and groups all around beneath the marquee and its glittering lights. Like so much of Merritt, the place looked frozen in time. Once inside, Jasmine stepped up to the box and spoke to the young man in the booth. Her tickets were in an enchanting embossed envelope which read “Jasmine Cline,” in a lovely delicate script.

The Lyric had once been an Opera house. Opulent scrolling woodwork and gilded extravagance of a time long passed surrounded. It was aging but still impressive. The ushers and staff were all wearing old fashioned uniforms. Royal purple with gold buttons and trim, topped with a small round cap. Young men dressed in this manner seemed to be everywhere. It added to the feeling they had stepped back in time. One such young man took their coats at the coat check counter and passed small tickets to Eric.

Jasmine caught sight of her mother hanging around some of the staff. Donna Cline sat on the board of non-profit which ran the theater. Jasmine was grateful her mom just gave her an approving look and stayed put. Eric knew her mom, of course, but a first date was no time to make small talk with your mother.

Eric held her hand as they wandered through the timeless theater. They found their seats, dead center in the 5th row. Jasmine peeked at the playbill. Musical Comedy of Murders was first played in the 1940s. It was a satire and not even a musical. Jasmine was sort of relieved to read that, community theaters were kind of hit or miss when it came to musicals.

The lights dimmed and she relaxed into her chair. Eric softly scooped up her fingers and wound his own through them.

The play was kind of a campy farce and occasionally hard to follow since the actors were playing actors and one woman seemed to be playing a set of interchangeable triplets. A group of actors was snowed in at a mansion owned by a German heiress. They had visited the mansion to audition for a film and of course, as the snow piled up, so did the bodies. The Stage Door slasher took out his victims and somehow the cast made these murders hilariously funny.

The dialogue was littered with silly banter and innuendos. The actors put on an impressive slapstick performance. Jasmine was captivated. At one point the lights went out through the entire theater. The characters could be heard crashing into one another and the audience roared with laughter. Suddenly the lights came up and one of the German sisters tripped over a body.

Lily positively sparkled as Nikki and at one point she and a slew of characters spent several minutes chasing each other from hidden passageway to revolving bookcases and back again, trying to murder one another. The entire auditorium laughed and cheered their way through the show, and at curtain call, everyone leaped to their feet, shouting their bravos.

The cast came out a few at a time; supporting characters first, people who'd been murdered halfway through, and finally Lily Day and her husband Sam. The stage crew and the director came out and gave the leading women huge bouquets of roses. As a group, they all took a final bow and slipped back behind the curtain. People started to gather in small groups to chat about the play as they walked out.

Eric turned to Jasmine and extended a hand. Jasmine slipped her hand into his again and as he gently tugged her along, her heels made her pitch forward into him. They laughed together.

"Lily asked me to come and say hello backstage. Come with me?" Jasmine steadied herself.

"With pleasure," he answered.

The pair made their way into the dark corridors beyond the stage. Here, the lux design fell away; simple wood beams lined the walls. In many places wires and pipes were exposed, revealing the structure's age.

They passed several large shared dressing rooms and in the far left hall corner, a door was open. A couple seemed to be kissing in the doorway, though it was difficult to make out in the dim light. As they approached, it was clear that Sam and Lily were sharing a celebratory moment. Suddenly another woman's voice could be heard from within the room.

"Excuse me!" The young actress who had played Helsa Wenzel and a couple of other characters emerged between the happy couple, almost shoving them out of her way. She seemed shocked to see Eric and Jasmine standing in the hall. Eric moved Jasmine out of the way with one strong arm.

"Uh, I um, I'm sorry." The small actress murmured and hurried off with a flimsy wave. The two couples chuckled together and the women shared a hug.

"I'm so glad you came. What did you think?" Lily sunk back into her husband's arms.

"Oh I just loved it, you were both wonderful. When do you leave for Hollywood?" Jasmine smiled at the actors.

"Well, as soon as I can talk this one into it that is the plan." Sam gave his wife a little squeeze and she beamed up at him.

"We'll see," Lily responded and gazed up into Sam's eyes. The sultry way they mooned at each other made Jasmine feel like maybe she and Eric had interrupted something.

"Well, Eric and I just wanted to congratulate you on a great show. We should probably get home, huh?" She asked Eric and he gave her a knowing look.

"Yes, we'd better go. Great opening night you two. Try not to forget us little people, when you hit it big," he said with a wink. The group all laughed together again and parted ways.

Jasmine and Eric chatted cheerfully on the drive back to Jasmine's cottage.

"I can't remember the last time I saw a play," Eric commented, "thank you that was fun."

'It was, wasn't it? I admit I didn't have high expectations but they did put on a fantastic show. I wonder what they're doing for the Christmas season." Jasmine remembered her mother mentioning a play was scheduled for the holiday season. She thought auditions were just a week or so away.

"Whatever it is, I hope you'll come see it with me." Eric smiled without averting his eyes from the road.

"Me too," Jasmine said as they pulled up in front of her sweet little house. She was wistful about the end of the night. The end! Suddenly her stomach fluttered. She realized they'd say goodbye in a moment. Would they kiss? Should they? Ack. Her mind raced. Eric hopped out of the car and came around to open her door. He extended a hand to help her out of the vehicle. Somehow, when she slipped her hand into his, all those nerves fell away.

Eric tugged her gently up and out of the vehicle and she found herself face to face with him in the cool night air. He gazed down at her with those kind, deep blue eyes. She took a deep breath and closed her eyes. She felt Eric's soft warm lips press into her own. Her heart skipped a beat and she inhaled, Eric's cedar scent swirled around her. When he stepped back, he still held her hand and walked with her to the front door. Once she'd unlocked the door and stepped inside Eric smiled again and pressed his lips against her cheek.

He whispered, "Night, Jazz." He closed the door himself and Jasmine watched him stride down her stairs and walkway. She stood there breathlessly and watched as he drove off.

Jasmine realized she'd been standing there gawking for a few moments. She shook her head and giggled at herself. She flicked on the lights and stepped out of her heels. She hung up her coat and as she scooped up her heels and wandered back toward her room she replayed that kiss in her head, perhaps too many times, as she dozed off.

CHAPTER FIVE

Jasmine woke that Saturday morning to a cheerful woman's voice singing "Walking on Sunshine." She opened her eyes and glanced at her phone. Six am Saturday, October 7th. The little weather icon on her home screen had clouds drifting across the cartoon sun. She smiled brightly and stretched. Saturday mornings were usually dedicated to trail running, and an overcast October morning was absolutely perfect for a long run.

She got up and danced around her room, enjoying the music while straightening the bed and getting dressed. She slicked her hair back into a high ponytail and tightened her running shoes. Jasmine stepped out onto her back porch and inhaled deeply. The air was cool and clean. It smelled ever so slightly of damp leaves. She did a series of stretches and warmed up her muscles before bouncing down the stairs. One of her favorite things about her new home was its proximity to a series of trails in the Superior National Forest. She could choose different routes for a change of scenery or intensity. Today she decided to run the Lookout Mountain Trail. It was more a hill than a mountain but she convinced herself the elevation would make up for some of those pastries she'd indulged in.

As she got into her groove Jasmine's mind wandered back to her date with Eric Canton last night. She almost felt silly for having been so nervous about it. It had been so easy and comfortable to spend the evening with him. Most first dates were filled with awkward conversations and even more awkward silences. She didn't recall any awkward moments from last night. She did, however, remember plenty of shared laughter and lingering glances. His hand at her waist or clasped around hers, guiding her through rooms that seemed both empty, and filled with watching eyes. And of course…. That kiss. Gentle and passionate, Eric's kiss made her head swim. It had made her heart race as first kisses should, but it also felt… familiar. Like coming home after a long trip.

Jasmine grinned. She reached the Lookout and took a moment to enjoy the view. A vast wooded valley lay between her and the opposite hill which she thought was called Hull Rust. The trees were all fading into beautiful crimsons and shades of gold. She imagined all the tourists would be very pleased with the fall colors during the upcoming festival. The festival would bring tastier, more tempting treats to threaten her waistline. She shrugged to herself. Oh well, she could just run this trail a few more times and enjoy this view while it lasted.

When she returned home Jasmine clicked on the news and slipped into a long hot shower. She put on a soft oversized cream colored sweater and leggings before stepping into some furry slippers. She brewed herself a cup of coffee and made some toast and scrambled eggs. She was enjoying her coffee and breakfast in front of the TV when something the news anchorwoman said caught her attention.

"The dog appears to be tangled in the barbed wire at the edge of town." A camera at the scene showed a large tan dog being held down and stroked by several people. "First responders and local police are trying to keep him calm to prevent further injury. As you can see the poor thing is quite scratched up already." The pretty blonde newswoman turned to her co-host and said, "I hope they can help him, Scott. Poor thing."

Jasmine was on her feet before she hear Scott's response. She threw on a light coat and traded her slippers for her tall boots. She grabbed her keys and ran out the door. She glanced briefly at the back seat of her Jeep before hopping in. She was relieved to she'd left her med case in her Jeep. Jasmine knew just where that news team had been filming that poor dog. There was a stretch of old barbed wire fence at the far end of last streets of Merritt, where the town ended and farmland began. She bypassed the main streets of town by taking the highway around and arrived less than fifteen minutes after she'd first seen the news report.

In addition to a police car and two medical vehicles, a small crowd had gathered. They watched from a safe distance as a policeman Jasmine recognized to be Greg Tucker and a couple of first responders tried to keep the dog from struggling. The poor dog was whining pitifully as Jasmine walked up. She noticed one of the men was holding a large set of wire cutters, but the dog was so frantic he couldn't get a good enough grip on the wire to cut it without harming the animal.

"Hey Jazz," Greg said with a glance. "I wondered if I should call you."

"I guess you don't need to now." Jasmine kneeled next to him and opened her kit. She prepared a syringe. "You mind if I help our friend here take a quick nap?"

"You're a lifesaver Jazz." Officer Tucker nodded. The dog seemed to be a Pitbull mix and very strong, the men were struggling to keep him still, and mostly failing. The poor dog wasn't being aggressive or mouthy; he just seemed frightened and desperate to be free from the barbs poking him.

Jasmine managed to poke the syringe into a muscular haunch. The dog yelped but settled down almost immediately. Within moments he was sound asleep. The fellow with the wire cutter got to work snipping away the thick, rusted barbed wire. Jasmine got a better look at the pooch. He seemed a little on the thin side. One or two of his lacerations looked serious and may need stitches, but most of them looked superficial.

"Any idea where he came from?" She stood and asked the young police officer.

"No idea, there are no tags on his collar, but he looks like he hasn't eaten much lately." Greg was perceptive. He and Jasmine had attended high school around the same time. She seemed to remember him in a football jersey, which he'd traded out for a uniform and badge these days.

"Poor guy," Jasmine replied absently.

The first responders managed to clip the unconscious dog from his self-made trap.

"What do ya want us to do with him now?" one of the men asked Greg. Greg looked to Jasmine.

“Um, why don’t you bring him to my shop? He may need stitches, and he should have a tetanus shot. I’ll meet you there.” She answered with confidence.

It was then that Jasmine realized she was being filmed. A cameraman was laser focused on her and suddenly a young woman with a microphone was standing before her.

“Dr. Cline, isn’t it? How did you calm that dog down so easily?” The young woman asked aloud. She mouthed to Jasmine, “Live TV,” and gestured to the camera.

“Uh...Uhm. I gave him a mild tranquilizer. He’s sound asleep now but he’ll be awake again in a couple of hours.” Jasmine tried to sound confident now but the camera made her suddenly nervous.

“It’s good news for him, then. Dr. Cline, do you think the poor pup will be alright?”

“Well he still needs a full examination, but my first impression is that his injuries are mostly skin deep. With some rest and a tetanus shot, I think he’ll recover quickly.” Jasmine smiled weakly at the camera.

“Thanks so much for your time Doctor. I’ll let you get back to it. Great work!” She turned to the camera. Jasmine sighed heavily with relief as the camera swung away from her to focus on the journalist.

“There you have it, folks, barbed wire couldn’t hold this bowwow down. The crew at KBRT would like to give a big thank you to the first responders here on site, to the Merritt Valley Police Department, and the Dr. Cline of the Merritt Valley Mobile Veterinary Clinic! Back to you the station, Mary.”

As the cameraman went back to the news van, the young woman with the mic turned to Jasmine.

“Say, sorry about that. Normally I would ask before pushing a live camera on someone. I’m Nancy Vale.” She extended a hand.

Jasmine accepted the handshake. “Well, you gave us a nice plug at the end there so I guess it’s a fair trade. It’s okay. I should get going though; the dog does need some care right away.”

“Oh of course. Say, you think I could stop by your shop and follow up in a couple of days? People eat up feel-good dog stories with a happy ending.” Nancy asked.

“Uh, sure. See you then.” Jasmine turned and hurried to her Jeep.

She arrived at the shop just as the medics’ van pulled into the back parking lot. The larger of the two men scooped up the dog in a blanket, still deeply asleep. Inside, he laid the pooch on am exam table.

“Even hurt, he seemed real sweet; I don’t think he’s a biter.” The man mentioned as Jasmine pulled out a muzzle.

“I’m sure you’re right, just standard procedure,” Jasmine answered and as he waved goodbye she slid the muzzle in place. She didn’t think he was a biter, either. Her phone rang.

“Jazz are you okay?” Claire seemed to be in a wind tunnel.

“I’m fine thanks, are you in a hurricane?”

Claire laughed. “I’m on my way into work; I figured you could use a hand.”

“Oh good see you in a few then.” Jasmine hung up and set her phone on the desk.

When Claire arrived they cleaned and dressed the nameless dog's wounds. He only needs seven stitches. They also checked for a microchip but didn't find one. He got updated shots and his nails trimmed while he slept. Jasmine was just starting to wonder if she'd misjudged his weight before she dosed his tranquilizer when he started to stir. His tail started to wag before he even opened his eyes.

They got him up on his feet and walked him into the fenced area behind the shop. He seemed happy as could be, you'd have no idea he was stuck in a barbed-wire tangle only 3 hours earlier.

"No owner, no microchip. Should I call the shelter?" Claire asked and patted the pup's head. His tail wagged immediately and he licked her hand as best he could in a muzzle.

"Hm. Well, I don't want him healing on a cold concrete floor. I… maybe I'll take him home with me." Jasmine thought aloud.

"Well, try not to fall in love with him, in case his family turns up. Hey, speaking of looooove how was your date last night? Claire bumped Jasmine with an elbow.

"Honestly? It was sort of fantastic." Jasmine led their no-name friend back inside.

"Sort of fantastic? That's all I'm going to get?" Claire teased.

"I mean. It was better than any first date I've been on. It was fun and romantic. Eric was a total gentleman and boy, does he clean up nice." Jasmine felt her cheeks flush. She took a few sample packets of dog food out of a drawer and popped them in her bag.

"I bet he does. He doesn't look too shabby in farm gear, either. Does this mean there will be a second date?" Claire was giddy. She was perpetually single, married to her work.

"I hope so," Jasmine replied. "He did say he hopes I'll go see the Christmas play with him."

"Well, I hope it doesn't take you guys two more months to go out again," Claire said playfully. She pulled on her fleece jacket and started to turn out the lights. "You sure you wanna take this big guy home with you?" Claire nodded toward the unnamed pooch.

"Yeah, I think he's been on his own long enough." Jasmine scratched his head. "I guess we better come up with something to call you, huh buddy?"

"Uh oh. Careful." Claire smiled. Dogs were so easy to love.

The two vets parted ways. Claire locked up and Jasmine coaxed her new friend into the back seat. He sat back easily enough. She wondered how such a well-behaved dog had ended up alone in the woods.

It had been a few years since Jasmine had had a dog. Between veterinary school, then working long hours for Lee Hwan, and all the hard work it had taken to open the clinic, there just hadn't been time. A small part of her hoped this dog's family wouldn't turn up looking for him, but Monday she'd make sure the local pet rescue had all his information and some photos to help find them.

Jasmine felt a hot breath on her neck. She turned and the dog licked her face from the back seat. She giggled.

"Well, what should we call you, huh? Rex? Max? Pete?" In response, the dog panted happily.

"Hm. What about, Francis? I could call you Frank for short. What do you think…? Francis?" She added some flare to the name and the dog perked up. "Okay, Francis it is then."

They arrived home and Francis followed Jasmine inside like he'd been there all along. She stashed her sample dog food in the cupboard above the closet. Francis would at least have breakfast. Tomorrow, she'd have to go to the feed store and pick up some things. Breakfast! She had forgotten all about the breakfast she'd started some hours ago. She turned to find Francis sitting next to her plate on the table. He looked pretty interested in the old toast and eggs but hadn't touched it. Jasmine smiled. "Good boy."

She grabbed the plate and her coffee cup. Francis followed her to the kitchen. She slid the eggs onto the floor for him and he gobbled them up. Jasmine didn't like to give dogs people food but knew that eggs were a healthy exception. The extra protein would do him good while he was healing anyhow.

After she cleaned up breakfast and made herself a quick sandwich, she curled up on the couch. Francis found a spot on the floor. Jasmine flipped channels for a while before pulling a soft throw over herself and dozing off.

When she woke, Francis had managed to find a place at the other end of the couch. His head was lying on Jasmine's legs. She looked down at him and maybe she should have been annoyed that he was on her furniture, but he gazed back up at her with sweet sad brown eyes and she just couldn't be upset. Maybe Claire was right, she was in danger of falling in love twice this weekend.

It was early evening. The light streaming in through the windows was weak; the sun must be near setting. She stretched out an arm and turned on the table lamp. Francis would need to go out and she desperately wanted to brush her teeth. She stretched again and just as she was about to swing her feet on the floor, she caught a glimpse of herself on the screen.

The scroll beneath her read, "Local vet saves trapped dog." Her name appeared below the image of her talking to Nancy Vale. She was relieved to see that she looked okay, even in her comfortable Saturday clothes and no makeup. They showed a clip of her crouched over Francis giving him the tranquilizer shot. Jasmine looked calm, competent, and professional. She breathed a sigh of relief.

Her phone immediately started to go off as text messages rolled in.

Claire sent, "Nice job on the free publicity!"

Her mom's message read, "OMG you looked great on the news. You saved that poor dog all by yourself! Are you okay!? I'm so proud of you. Mom." Jasmine chuckled to herself.

Eric Canton sent, "Nice work with the dog, beautiful." Beautiful, huh? That was new.

Ellie and Brian sent texts as well as a few patients. The Bentons, too. Goodness, for a few minutes Jasmine felt positively famous. She set her phone aside. All those messages could wait. She got up and asked Francis if he'd like to go for a walk. He hopped off the couch and gave an enthusiastic wag of the tail in response. She clipped the leash to his collar, which she noticed was pretty ripped up from his adventures. She'd get him a new one of those, tomorrow, too. They went out the back door together. The wind was bitter cold tonight. Jasmine wasn't the only one to notice, Francis shivered visibly. He had a short coat and being a little underweight was doing him no favors. They made quick work of the walk, up the trail a bit and back.

Once inside, Jasmine took off her coat and turned on a few more lights, and lit the candles on her mantle. She enjoyed mood lighting and this room, in particular, had a nice glow with the right lighting. She got a few things started for dinner and poured herself a glass of white wine. She changed into a long soft nightdress with a matching robe. Francis followed her from room to room.

Jasmine finally settled back onto the couch with her wine and a bowl of homemade pasta with white sauce and oyster mushrooms. Francis didn't beg, he just lay down at her feet. Jasmine smiled. He might make a nice roommate, after all.

She enjoyed her meal, though it briefly crossed her mind that it's sort of lonely to eat dinner in front of the TV. She shrugged and sipped her wine, sitting back. She picked up her phone again. She supposed she had held off on responding to her messages long enough.

She answered Claire first, "Thanks, that was my plan all along!"

She answered everyone else with friendly thank yous and things like, "Just doing my job!"

Finally, she answered Eric's message;

"Thanks, mister. How's your night?"

"Better now. What are you up to?" Eric answered immediately.

"Just hanging out with my new friend," Jasmine snapped a picture of Francis curled up in front of the coffee table and hit send.

"He looks cozy. Dinner by candlelight, huh? Looks like I've got some competition."

"LOL, maybe. He is pretty handsome." Jasmine joked.

"I'm up to the challenge ;)" Eric retorted emoji and all. Jasmine sent back a wink emoji and set her phone aside. She could feel herself smiling like an idiot but it didn't bother her in the slightest. She flipped through the channels. She usually watched mysteries, Animal Planet, or maybe cooking shows, but tonight she settled on a silly romantic comedy. She enjoyed it more than she usually would. Possibly a good-looking farm vet in her inbox had something to do with that.

When the movie ended it was nearly eleven pm. Jasmine turned off the TV and set her remote down. She glanced down at Francis who had been snoring happily throughout the film. He looked up at her and stood up. His jowls were droopy, and yet, Jasmine could swear he was smiling at her.

"You wanna go outside before bed? Huh?" Francis woofed what could only mean yes, please? Jasmine was tempted to take him out without a leash, but given the way they'd met, she thought better of it. They stepped out into the backyard together. While Francis sniffed every leaf and pebble in the yard, Jasmine could swear she heard sirens in the distance, which wasn't common in Merritt.

Once inside, Jasmine turned out all the lights, blew out the lingering candles on the mantle, and headed to bed. She dug around in the back of her closet and found an old pillow for Francis who never seemed to be far behind her. She set it on the floor near her bed and patted it until he curled up on it. He almost fit, but he'd definitely need a bigger dog bed. She stroked his head and he just gazed at her until he drifted off.

She slipped between the sheets and was soon fast asleep, herself.

When Jasmine woke up Sunday morning, her phone was playing some 70's dance music. She stretched her whole body, arms up, legs out and her left leg brushed something warm and heavy. There was Francis, curled up as if he always slept on the bed with humans. Jasmine chuckled.

"You know, we're going to have to sit down and talk about some boundaries. You're too big to be on my furniture, young man." She scolded playfully. She got up and shooed him off the bed. He hopped down without protest and watched while she straightened her bedding and tossed his pillow back into the closet. Jazz got quickly into her running gear. She considered bringing Francis out running with her but decided against it, he had stitches and she wanted to get in an extra couple miles today. She took him out in the backyard and then closed him in her porch. So far he'd given her no reason to suspect he'd get into mischief if she left him loose in the house, but better not test that theory today.

She hit the trail just after 6:30 am. It was still pretty chilly out, wind whistled through the leaves. Jasmine cranked up her music and got into a groove. There were quite a few people already out, enjoying the fall colors. Jasmine guessed quite a few people were already in town for the Festival of Leaves.

Merritt Valley's small-town festivals drew in a fair share of tourists from larger cities. People who craved a taste of the idyllic small town life they probably only saw on TV. In addition to tourists, however, many people who had once lived in Merritt Valley and moved to those larger cities often came home for the festivals, the Festival of Leaves in particular. The surrounding orchards and active farms made harvest time especially appealing, with a huge farmer's market, and of course, people came to watch their nephews play in the Homecoming game, or see their relatives in grand march at the big dance.

Naturally, people from urban areas loved to take in the changing foliage on these trails. Jasmine ran past half a dozen people with huge cameras and several families just out for a morning hike. She saw a fair few other runners, too, including one she swore was an actress in the play she and Eric had attended Friday night. As the petite brunette approached, Jasmine squinted to get a better look. Yes, she was pretty sure that was the little actress who had been trapped in Lily Day's dressing room while Lily and Sam canoodled in the doorway. Just as Jasmine raised a hand to wave, the woman turned onto another branch of the trail.

Jasmine wondered about that briefly. That was an intense trail; it had a steep incline, wasn't paved, and had lots of roots and stones to navigate around. Jasmine was a seasoned trail runner, and even she usually avoided that one unless the scale had crept up a few digits.

Jasmine glanced down the trail as she passed it. The actress had completely vanished, so she must have been up to the challenge.

Jasmine completed a full six miles before she hit her back steps. She stopped to get a good stretch and Francis popped up, standing on his hind legs to peek out the window of the back door. Naughty. Jasmine laughed and went inside.

"Miss me?" She crouched down to pat him and he slurped her cheek.

Jasmine pulled out the little bags of dog food. She realized she didn't own dog dishes so she poured them into an old mixing bowl and filled another with water. She set them down next to the door to the back porch. Francis started to crunch away at his food happily. She got a chewable deramaxx out of her travel kit and found some sliced cheese to wrap it in. Dogs can't complain but she knew he must be sore with all those scratches and stitches. This was just a simple anti-inflammatory. When he'd finished his breakfast, Francis looked up at her.

"Sit?" Jasmine had no idea if he had any training. Francis wagged his tail and sat. To her surprise, he lifted a paw.

“Shake?” She took his paw and shook. That was a fun surprise. She offered the cheese with the pill inside with an open hand. He took it gently and it was gone in a flash.

“Good boy!” Francis wagged his tail again. He curled up near the couch. He must have been well-loved and cared for wherever he called home.

Jasmine took her time Sunday mornings. As a rule, she never watched the news or read the paper on Sundays. Sundays were to be enjoyed. She whipped up some blueberry pancakes and fresh coffee. She savored her breakfast at the kitchen table. Francis snored peacefully in the living room. She guessed his medication had kicked in and relieved his pain.

She took a long hot shower and slipped into buttery brushed jeans and an emerald green sweater. She didn’t fuss with her hair, it dried into neat ringlets. She put on her favorite tall boots. By the time she scooped up her purse and travel case, Francis was awake and sitting next to her. She clipped on his leash and they took off together.

He behaved beautifully while she ran errands. The first stop was the feed store, where they allowed pets. It was a huge warehouse where you could get anything from dog beds to fence panels. She chose a large grey fleece bed for Francis, along with a new matching collar and leash and some rich organic food that would help him get back up to a healthy weight in no time. She picked out some big porcelain bowls and a mat to set them on. She asked his approval on each selection, and he always wagged his tail in response. On a whim, Jasmine also used one of those automated machines to make him a name tag. It seemed strange to put her number on a tag for a dog that may go back home in a few days, but she thought it might be a good plan since he may have run off once already. She told herself it was for his safety, in case he got lost again.

She would have to leave him in the Jeep while she got groceries, so she cracked a window and hurried through the store. She was in and out in no time, with an armload of brown paper bags. She deposited them in the back on top of Francis’ supplies.

The route home took them down Grand Avenue. Jasmine wasn't surprised to see the street busy with people and traffic, but she was quite shocked to find police tape surrounding The Lyric Theatre. She was more surprised to find her mother talking to an officer just inside the police tape. Jasmine pulled up in front of the grand old building and hopped out with Francis.

"Oh, honey! Come here!" Donna Cline was as polished as ever but Jasmine could see her mom was upset. Her mom was a bit shorter than herself. She slipped into Jasmine's arms for a hug. "That's okay, isn't it? She's my daughter. She's a doctor!"

The officer nodded. "It's fine." Jasmine didn't recognize this policewoman. She resisted the urge to correct her mother and extended a hand. Donna and the rest of the town had a habit of saying doctor rather than veterinarian.

"Jasmine Cline." The detective reached out and shook her hand with a confident grip.

"Detective Williams. Is it Dr. Cline?" The detective had kind eyes but she was all business right now.

"Oh, I mean, yes technically, but I'm a veterinarian. Jasmine is fine." Jasmine didn't mean to sound as curt as she did.

"Very well Dr. Cline, did you know Lily Day?" Williams asked.

"I… not very well. I've treated her dog at the clinic." Jasmine paused. "*Did* I know her? Has something happened?" Jasmine didn't like Williams' tone at all.

"Mrs. Day was found dead in this theatre shortly after 10:30 pm last night." Williams was matter of fact.

"Isn't it just awful?" Donna Cline sniffled. "I had just hugged her a few minutes before. The play was wonderful last night. I just don't understand." She trailed off and Jasmine slipped an arm around her mom who was notably distraught.

"Do you have any idea what happened?" Jasmine directed her question to Detective Williams.

"Too soon to tell, but we'll certainly find out." A couple of uniformed officers and a young man with a large camera exited the front doors of the theatre.

"We've got everything we need." one of the officers said as they walked by.

"Great thanks," Williams answered. "Ms. Cline, will you see to it that this building stays locked? Does anyone else have keys?"

"Um. I think the director and stage manager do, and the maintenance man." Donna replied.

"I'd like all their phone numbers, please. You can text them to me at the number I gave you. Please let them know right away that no one is to enter. I'll be in touch." Williams nodded to them both and disappeared into her squad.

"I didn't even know Merritt Valley had a detective." Jasmine turned to her mom. "Are you okay? What on earth happened?"

"Oh I'll be alright but I wish I knew what happened. The show went so well, the theatre was nearly empty and then I heard a scream from backstage. It was Vicki Andrews, she played Helsa. Maybe you remember. Anyhow Vicki found Lily in her dressing room, dead!" Donna was quite shaken.

"Come on mom; let me get you some coffee. It's freezing out here." They walked toward the deli. "Why all the detectives and stuff? How did Lily die?"

"Honestly I have no idea. There was no blood or anything like that. But Sam kept saying his wife was murdered. He demanded the detective. I don't understand why, myself."

"Oh, that is weird. Oh mom I'm so sorry." They stopped in front of the deli and Jasmine hugged her mom. Donna Cline was not easily shaken.

"I better call everyone about not going into the theatre," Donna mentioned and dug her phone out of her purse.

"Here take Francis and I'll get us some coffee." Jasmine passed his leash over.

"Goodness, I hardly noticed him."

Jasmine ordered two coffees and some flakey apple pastries. Everyone inside seemed to be talking about Lily Day. Jasmine caught fragments of their conversations over the usual noise of a busy deli.

"Don't think Sam could hurt anybody," a woman whispered to her companion.

"It's so sad; she was so young and beautiful." Another woman murmured.

"What a waste, she was so talented. Saw that play Friday," a man mentioned.

"I doubt it was murder. There's never been a murder in Merritt, has there?" another whisper.

Jasmine was inclined to agree with that last one. Lily was so sweet and warm; Jasmine couldn't imagine she had had lots of enemies. Besides that, Jasmine was pretty sure there had never been a murder in Merritt.

She found her mom sitting at a table outside, a look of bewilderment on her face. She was finishing up a phone call and Francis was sitting beside her, his face on her leg.

"No, no one can go in, not even you Mark. Not until the police give us the word. Okay? It's alright the dirt will still be there in a few days." Donna said as Jasmine sat down. "Alright, thanks. I'll call you when it's okay. Say? You might hear from the detective, too. I don't know why. Alright. Goodbye."

"Are you sure you're okay?" Jasmine was concerned for her mom.

"Yes, yes. Just shocked by it all. I didn't get much rest." Donna replied.

"I believe it," Jasmine responded. Jack came out with their coffee and pastries. He set the tray on the table and patted Mrs. Cline's arm.

"Say, real sorry to hear about Lily, Mrs. Cline," Jack said earnestly.

"Thanks, Jack." Donna accepted her coffee thankfully and took a long sip. She seemed to suddenly notice Francis, whose head was still resting on her knee.

"What a good boy." Donna patted the dog's head. "You did such good work with him yesterday. With all the fuss I almost forgot about him. Where did he come from?"

"I'm not sure. We let a few local shelters know about him. Hopefully, we'll find his family. He's so well trained I can't believe someone somewhere isn't looking for him." Jasmine meant that even though she sort of wished he could stay with her.

"He's such a comfort." Donna was distracted petting the sweet dog.

"What's at the theatre that you can't go in?" Jasmine asked.

"I don't know. Evidence, I guess?" Donna seemed like she was weary of talking about Lily's untimely death. She changed topics. "Hey, I saw you with Eric Canton at Friday's show. How did that go?"

"Oh mom, it was wonderful. It was one of the best dates I've been on. He's so easy to talk to." She spoke candidly.

"Easy to look at, too. I noticed you had a new dress for the occasion. You like this one, don't you?" Mrs. Cline never missed anything.

"I really do. I never thought we'd end up dating but I'm pretty pleased we have. I'm excited about it." Jasmine answered and realized she should probably tell Eric about Lily. Later, she thought.

"Oh good, I've always liked Eric. He's kind, good-looking, smart, built a nice business for himself. He's got everything a girl should look for in a husband." Donna said with a matter of fact tone.

"Oh mom, let's not get ahead of ourselves." Jasmine chuckled and her mom finally smiled.

After she felt sure her mother could make it home safe on her own, Jasmine said her goodbyes and headed home with Francis. She wished he could help unload and put away all those groceries. She scooped up as much as she could but made a couple of trips. As she unpacked groceries and dog supplies, she couldn't help but wonder what had happened to poor Lily Day. It seemed like only hours ago she'd watched that vibrant young actress make the whole town laugh.

Jasmine set up Francis' new mat and dishes. She gave him some fresh water and poured some food for him. Since he was a little on the skinny side, she would feed him a few times daily until his weight leveled out. He gobbled up the kibble, tail wagging. She got herself a glass of water and sat down in front of the TV.

Nancy Vale was standing in front of the old Lyric Theatre. Jasmine hit mute just after Nancy reported that if Sam Day was right, this was the first murder in Merritt Valley in a hundred years. The scroll beneath Nancy mirrored Jasmine's thoughts.

"Why does Sam Day believe his wife was murdered?"

Indeed, it seemed very odd that despite no sign of violence or struggle, Sam assumed the worst. It was stranger still since the spouse was usually the top suspect in a homicide.

Jasmine didn't care to watch the local news people speculate. She flipped to some innocuous show about DIY home renovations and picked up her cell phone. There were a few messages from friends, probably wanting to gossip about Merritt's first murder in a century. Jasmine didn't feel up to that. She tapped on Eric's smiling face, a photo she'd snipped from his social media.

"Hey. How's my favorite vet?" Jasmine wondered if that was too friendly but hit send anyhow.

"Kinda bummed out honestly, how's my favorite vet?" Eric answered almost immediately.

"I'm okay, bummed, too. I guess you heard about Lily?"

"Yeah. I know we didn't know her but it's still sad." Eric replied. Jasmine suddenly felt teary. She had been keeping a stiff upper lip until now. In their work, they both saw births and deaths all the time. Lily was practically a stranger. It felt silly to cry over the death of a stranger, but Jasmine couldn't help it. Suddenly, she didn't want to be alone.

"It really is. Are you busy? I could use some company." Jasmine's heart skipped as she hit send.

"I'm not busy. See you in 30?" Again, he answered without hesitation.

"K." Jasmine set her phone down and rushed to her room. Francis followed. He took up watch at her bedroom door.

Jasmine sighed with relief when she saw herself in the mirror. Her hair had dried nicely, long ringlets falling all around her face and shoulders. She smoothed some soft berry-tinted gloss over her lips and a little mascara. She put on a caramel colored sweater over a beige tank, the earth tones played nicely with her deep olive skin. She spritzed on a soft floral scent and coaxed Francis out of the doorway. He seemed to take his guard duties very seriously.

She flipped on the lights and straightened up the living room. She considered for a moment and decided against lighting the candles. Too much, she thought. It had been 15 minutes since Eric had said to give him 30. Jasmine sat awkwardly on her couch for a moment before she hopped up and bounced to the kitchen. She took out some pre-cut chocolate chip cookie dough from the fridge, pulled out a cookie sheet, and popped half a dozen cookies in the oven. She set the temperature and timer. Who doesn't like fresh baked cookies when they're feeling down?

Jasmine had just perched on the couch when she heard a car door out front. Typically she would have waited for a knock or the doorbell. But she met Eric at the door. As she opened it, his face lit up. He was carrying a brown paper bag with twine handles. He skipped most of the stairs on his way up.

"Hey." was all Jasmine could manage.

"Hey," Eric answered. He slipped his free arm around her waist and pulled her toward him. He gave her a soft lingering kiss and hugged her. Jasmine rested there a moment. She hadn't realized how much she'd missed him.

Behind her, Francis gave a low bark.

"Oh, he is the competition." Eric joked. He stepped past Jasmine and offered a hand for Francis to sniff. "Hey, buddy."

"I've been calling him Francis." Jasmine shut the door behind them.

"Francis, huh? I think you mentioned that. Good looking dog. Boxer mix?" Francis seemed to approve of Eric's aroma and gave his hand a lick. Eric scratched the dog's head.

"I think so. Maybe pit? Whatever he is, he's got great house manners. Except he keeps getting on my bed."

"Who can blame him?" Eric said, almost under his breath. They chuckled together. "Hey, I brought some snacks. Kettle and caramel corn. Some of the food trucks are already open downtown." He offered the brown bag.

"Oh good. Those trucks will be the death of me." Jasmine realized too late that perhaps that phrase was ill-timed. She felt herself blush and dropped her eyes to the floor. Eric touched her cheek.

"It's okay, Jazz." He gave her such a sincere look. His endlessly blue eyes touched hers and everything else melted away.

A sudden beep beep beep came from the kitchen.

"The cookies!" Jasmine exclaimed. "I'll be right back." She hurried off to retrieve the cookies. She arranged them neatly on a plate, which she set on a tray with two small glasses of milk. When she returned to the living room she was pleased to find Eric lighting the candles on the mantle, Francis lying on the floor beside him. This was something she could get used to.

Eric reached for a cookie before she could set them down.

"I wondered what smelled so good." He took a bite and closed his eyes, smiling. Jasmine settled in next to him. He moved ever so slightly closer to her. She chose a cookie and took a bite herself.

"How's your mom handling things?" Eric asked before gulping some milk.

"Honestly, this is the first time I've seen her shaken up in a long time. She's usually so put together, you know?" Jasmine sipped her glass of milk.

"Seems to run in the family," Eric remarked. "What do the police think?"

"That's the funny thing about this. I stopped by the theatre earlier because my mom was there. There was a detective there, asking questions, but she also said there was no reason to believe there had been foul play."

"Then what was she doing there?" Eric placed his glass back on the tray and leaned back into the couch.

"When they found Lily, Sam kept repeating, 'My wife was murdered.'"

Eric considered this for a moment. "I wonder what's happening there."

"Me too." Jasmine curled up close to Eric and he curled his arm around her.

"Should we find a movie to watch?" Eric asked and reached for the remote.

"Yes, please." She was surprised when Eric settled on A Philadelphia Story. Most guys would have shied away from "chick flicks." Then again, Eric wasn't most guys.

The pair watched a few movies curled up together. After a Philadelphia Story, His Girl Friday came on and neither Eric nor Jasmine made a move to change the channel. Together, they snacked their way through most of the cookies, kettle corn, and caramel corn. They even took a break to make a plate of ham and turkey sandwiches for dinner.

Jasmine and Eric laughed and joked all the while. Jasmine hadn't enjoyed a night in like this in years. It was nearing ten pm Jasmine was curled up, her head resting on Eric's chest. She couldn't remember the name of the movie they were watching, but it didn't matter. The heroine and her hero kissed to dramatic music and the words, "The End," appeared in an elaborate font. As the end credits started to scroll, she felt Eric shift and kiss the top of her head. He stretched and made moves to get up so she shifted to give him space.

"Well, I guess I should get going. I had a great time tonight, Jazz. Thanks." He gazed at her a moment and stood up. Jasmine stood too and nearly tripped over Francis. They both laughed and Eric slipped into his wool pea coat.

"I had a great time, too. Thanks for coming over tonight." She saw him to the door and unlocked it.

"It was my pleasure." Eric touched her cheek with a few gentle fingertips. He bent to place the softest kiss upon her lips. There was a little more heat in this kiss. She felt him smile and she smiled too.

"Goodnight." He said in nearly a whisper.

"Night," Jasmine replied. She closed the door behind him. She almost felt guilty, she'd invited Eric over to keep her company after they'd both learned of Lily Day's untimely death, and yet it had been a beautiful evening home together. When Jasmine's father had passed away years earlier, her mother had said; "You can't honor the dead by giving up on your own life. You have to keep on going." Jasmine thought it was still excellent advice.

She sighed and tidied up, picking up plates and cups from her movie night with Eric. Francis followed behind and was awarded wayward popcorn that fell as she carried the tray to the kitchen. She made quick work of washing up the dishes and popped outside with Francis before bed.

Jasmine showed Francis his new bed under the window in her bedroom. He gave it a good sniff and sat down. He just stared at her. She patted the doggie bed. He looked at the bed, then back at her. She chuckled.

"Well, maybe you'll try it sometime."

Jasmine slid into the sheets and sunk into deep pillows. Her mind wandered. She thought about her evening with Eric Canton. He was easy to spend time with and easier to talk to. It felt like talking to an old, dear friend. Though, when he kissed her, well. She didn't have any friends who made her feel like that. She wanted to take her time with Eric but she genuinely couldn't wait to see him again.

Jasmine wondered if this is how people fell in love. Of course, she had dated in school but it had never felt so comfortable or natural. She remembered clumsy dates and clunky first kisses. All the women's magazines said relationships worked best when they were built upon friendship. Jasmine didn't want to get ahead of herself, but so far whoever, "they," were seemed to be right about that. Eric had been her friend for years.

Then she wondered how Sam and Lily Day had met. How did they fall in love? Maybe they had spent Sunday afternoons practicing lines and making dinners together. Maybe they'd spent nights curled up together on the couch, watching murder mysteries and daydreaming together about Hollywood ambitions.

Murder mysteries. Jasmine wondered if Lily's death was indeed a mystery to be solved. Had her death been an accident? A heart attack? Maybe she had a tragic health condition no one knew about.

Or, had Lily been murdered, as her husband Sam suggested? That thought led to so many other questions. How do you kill someone without any sign of attack or injury? Had she perhaps been poisoned? And most importantly, who would have reason to poison her? Who would murder Lily Day?

CHAPTER SIX

Jasmine Cline woke to her alarm at 6 am Monday. She stretched and glanced over at Francis' new plaid dog bed. It was empty. She sat up and found Francis fully stretched out at the foot of the bed. She shook her head.

"Beds are for people!" She scolded playfully. Francis lifted his head to look at her but did not seem concerned. He lay back down and resumed sleeping. Jasmine chuckled and hopped out of bed.

She showered quickly and got ready for the day. She'd spend today in the office so she dressed comfortably in a long brushed jersey blouse, leggings, and soft hiking boots. She smoothed back her curls in a high bun and skipped the makeup. She started the coffee pot and poured Francis' breakfast while it brewed. She would have a breakfast bar on the road today so she just watched him gobble up his kibble.

"You wanna come to work with me today?" He wagged his tail in response. Jasmine didn't want to leave him home for long hours and at the office, she could put some ointment on his scratches. She clipped his leash on, slipped on an oversized wool coat and they were off.

There were a few extra cars parked on her street this morning. Jasmine guessed many of her neighbors must have out-of-town company for the Festival of Leaves. A few people waved from the sidewalks as she and Francis rolled down the drive in her Jeep.

They arrived downtown to find Merritt's main street transformed. The sidewalks were filled with people as if the small town's population had tripled overnight. Tourists were already enjoying pastries and muffins at The Muffin Man and a few young women seemed to be taking selfies in front of the display tractor which was surrounded by straw bales, pumpkins, and corn husks. Hashtag pumpkin spice latte, hashtag the Festival of Leaves. Jasmine laughed aloud at her own joke and Francis cocked his head.

Jasmine passed the Lyric Theater and noted that the police tape was gone. She pulled around and parked in the back lot where Brian was stringing up ropes. He greeted Jasmine and Francis with a wave.

"Good morning Brian. What's with the rope?"

"Oh, some people were parking here when I got in. I figured we might need some signs." Brian passed her a pile of signs that read Customer Parking Only.

"Smart thinking. Thanks, Brian." Jasmine passed the signs back and headed inside with Francis in tow.

"Morning Ellie." She surprised their office administrator.

"Well Jeez, morning boss. Where'd you come from? Who's this?" Ellie crouched to stroke Francis' head and was rewarded with a sloppy dog kiss.

"Meet Francis. We found him tangled in the barbed wire at the end of town."

"Oh you know, I saw that! What a nice boy you are, huh?" Ellie and Francis made fast friends.

"What's in the book for me today?" Jasmine inquired.

"Um let's see." Ellie flipped open the schedule on her desktop. "Pretty quiet day. A couple of puppy checkups and a pregnant guinea pig this afternoon. It's kind of slow all week; I guess people are busy with the Festival of Leaves."

"That's alright after last week I don't mind a few slow days."

"True! Hey, did you hear about that poor actress?" Ellie's usual bright expression dimmed.

"I did. So sad, I liked her." Jasmine replied.

"Me, too." Ellie turned to her computer so Jasmine headed to the med room. She got some more anti-inflammatories out and noted it on a form. She popped one chewable Deramaxx out of the bottle and dug out some pill treats. She slipped the pill into a bacon flavored treat and got down to Francis' level.

"Sit." Francis sat.

"Shake?" He handed her a paw for a shake.

"Lay down." Francis obliged.

"Good boy." Jasmine was ever impressed by her new friend. He took the treat gently from her hand. Of course, he left behind ample slobber, but that couldn't be helped.

"When Brian finishes up we'll take a look at those stitches." The stitches were on his lower ribs and stomach; she'd need him on the exam table to get a good look.

"Hey, you," Claire called from the door.

"Morning Claire. How are you this morning?" Jasmine inquired.

"Great except it's only Monday and it's nearly a zoo outside." Claire scoffed.

"Hey, a zoo would be great for business." Jasmine joked.

"Okay, but you take the ones with the big teeth." The two women giggled. "How's our new friend?"

"He's doing great. A little sore. Hey maybe you can help me pick up him, I want to look at those stitches."

"Sure," Claire answered. Together they gently lifted the big dog and set him on the table. They looked him over and swabbed some antibacterial ointment on the cuts that needed it.

"What's on your schedule today?" Jasmine asked Claire as they set Francis back on his feet.

"I think just a cat who needs updated shots and Mr. Lind's overweight beagle. How about you?" Claire asked in return.

"A pregnant guinea pig and a couple of puppy checkups," Jasmine answered.

"I guess maybe you're right about the zoo." Claire chuckled. "Buy you lunch later? We can be the local color for all the tourists," she quipped.

"It's a date." Jasmine smiled.

Jasmine stopped in her office with Francis, since she had a few minutes before her first appointment. She checked her phone and found a couple of new messages. One from her mother read, "Call me later, Mom." It always made Jasmine smile that her mom signed her texts.

The other message was from Eric. Jasmine smiled and flipped it open.

It was a picture from "His Girl Friday," one of the black and white romances they had watched together last night. The white text over it read, "Good morning."

Jasmine grinned. She tapped off a quick text to him that read, "Good morning, mister. Have a great day." She felt those butterflies in her stomach again and laughed at herself. Maybe she was being ridiculous but she didn't mind.

She turned to Francis. "Stay here. I'll be back." He seemed to understand; he lay down beside her desk and sighed audibly. Jasmine knew he'd get some good rest with the medication in his system.

On her way to exam room 2 she stopped at the front desk.

"Hey Ellie, let everyone know that Francis is in my office. I'm sure he'll be fine but I haven't had a chance to assess his aggression with other pets, so it's best if he stays in there for now."

"Okay, Dr. Cline!" Ellie chimed over a stack of books. Ellie was working on her degree online.

A young woman around Ellie's age greeted Jasmine in exam room two. She had five lovely Australian Shepherd puppies playfully chomping each other around her feet. Jasmine extended a hand.

"Good morning, I'm Jasmine Cline." she smiled.

"Hi, I'm Robin." The young lady replied.

"And what brings you all in today?" Jasmine often asked patients questions she knew the answer to.

"These little guys are almost ready for new homes. I wanted to do their first shots and checkups before I send them off." Robin lifted one puppy and kissed his tiny nose.

"I think we can take care of that. Beautiful puppies." Jasmine opened her hands to signal she was ready for a pup and Robin obliged, passing one over to her.

"Thanks, their mom and dad are both agility champions. I'm going to keep this one, I think." Robin motioned to the little white and speckled fluff ball on the exam table.

“You look like a champion too,” Jasmine said to the puppy, rather than to Robin.

She looked over all the pups to check for mites, skin infections, or any abnormalities. Everyone got shots and treats, and she taught Robin how to brush their teeth. The pups were not pleased about the shots but puppies forget fast and she watched all the little tails wagging as she left Robin to wrangle them up and get them back in their carrier.

Next up, pregnant guinea pig. In exam room four, a burly gentleman greeted her bruskly. Jasmine thought he might look more comfortable on a motorcycle than here in her office, holding a very large guinea pig.

“Hi Ma’am I’m Tom.” He said without getting up.

“Hello Tom, I’m Jasmine Cline. And this is?” Jasmine nodded to his furry companion.

“Dolly Pardon.” He had a slight southern accent.

“Well, it’s nice to meet you both. Maybe I can have you place Dolly on the table for me.” Jasmine picked up the chart and looked over the notes.

“8 weeks pregnant, hm?” Jasmine asked Tom and he nodded. “You’ve been feeding her alfalfa? Peppers and kale?” He nodded again. “Very good, she needs those extra nutrients and vitamin c.” Jasmine made a few notes and set aside her pad. She ran her fingers gingerly over Dolly’s sides and stomach, then her undercarriage.

“Feels like 5 pups, and it feels like her pelvic bones are shifting properly for labor. Try not to pick her up unless it’s absolutely necessary, and when you do, make sure you support her hips. Like this.” Jasmine lifted the guinea pig to demonstrate.

"When she goes into labor she'll let you know. She'll sort of yell. The pups will each have their own amniotic sac which she will probably remove and eat. If you notice a pup with a sac still over its face, gently tear it with your fingernail. Okay?" Jasmine glanced up at Tom and realized he was taking notes.

"Okay," Tom replied without looking up from his notes.

"If labor takes much more than 20 minutes, call us, she'll need medical intervention." Jasmine noticed Tom's eyes widen.

"Intervention? Does that happen a lot?" He asked with a concerned tone.

"Most births happen without issue, but in the case that it happens I want you to call us, okay?" Tom nodded again. "Ellie will give you a card with some information and our 24-hour number. Guinea pigs usually birth during daylight, but I want you to feel free to call that number any time, okay Tom?"

"Okay. Dolly means everything to Ginny." Tom looked over his notes, ensuring he hadn't missed something.

"Ginny?" Jasmine asked.

"My little girl, Ginny. She's 7."

"Ah. Well, you can let Ginny know that Dolly is doing great."

"Okay, thanks Doc," Tom answered sincerely but that look of concern didn't leave his face.

Jasmine made a few more notes and left Tom fussing over Dolly. She briefly pitied his wife; he must have been a mess when she had Ginny.

Jasmine found Francis still asleep next to her desk. She knew he needed rest, healing was really taking it out of him. She gave him a pat. He let out a heavy contented sigh. Jasmine updated her charts and tidied up some paperwork. She tapped her pen on the desk. She had never been any good at sitting around waiting.

She opened a browser on her computer and Googled Lily Day Merritt Valley Minnesota. A few articles popped up in the search so she chose the newest one, which had been published about a half-hour ago.

The article restated all the things Jasmine already knew. Lily had been found dead shortly after a performance Saturday night. She had no sign of injury and the police had no obvious reasons to suspect foul play. Her husband Samuel Day believed she had been murdered. Sam was quoted; "I know someone killed my Lily. I just know it. We need to find her killer!"

The article also revealed some information Jasmine hadn't been aware of. Sam Day was a local boy; he'd grown up in Merritt Valley and graduated from Merritt Valley high. As most Merritt Valley students did, Sam had moved to Minneapolis for college and that's where he'd met Lily. They had both performed small parts at some of the Twin Cities' renowned theatres. They had moved back to Merritt Valley temporarily, where the cost of living was lower. They had intended to work and save up with hopes of moving to Los Angeles or New York City to more seriously pursue their acting.

The end of the article read that while Lily's exact cause of death was unknown, but a detective on the case said she appeared to have suffocated. An autopsy would be performed and funeral plans were pending, awaiting the arrival of Lily's parents.

Jasmine leaned back in her chair. How does a person suffocate in a dressing room, without foul play? Jasmine played with a stray curl and considered the possibilities. Of course, one could choke on something, like a piece of hard candy or a chunk of meat. Jasmine didn't think there were steaks in the dressing rooms at the Lyric.

She smoothed the curl back in place. What about asphyxiation or anaphylaxis? Either could be caused by a chemical reaction or allergy. A light went off in Jasmine's head. An allergy. Hadn't Lily mentioned a serious equine allergy, right here in this office? It had been a few days since her exposure from Jasmine's coveralls so that hadn't killed her. However, if she'd been exposed to some horsehair or dander since then and left untreated... Yes, that could have killed her.

But that raised another question.

How would Lily have been exposed to a horse in the back of a playhouse?

Jasmine picked up her phone. It only rang once after she dialed.

"Jazz! How's my girl?" Donna Cline sounded like she was feeling better already.

"I'm great mom, how are you?"

"Oh just fine. I was just watching one of those cooking shows you like."

"Oh, nice. Say, mom? Did the police say you can go back inside the theatre yet?" Jasmine tried to sound nonchalant.

"Well, that Detective Williams called earlier to ask if I'll let her in today. She wants to make sure they got all the right pictures for their investigation. She said we should be able to enter after that. This is good because we've got tours all week and the show… I don't know what we're going to do about the show but it has to go on, doesn't it. How come?" Donna asked.

"There's something I'm curious about. You mind if I take a peek in the dressing room after the Detective says it's okay?" Jasmine asked.

"I… well no I don't mind. Wha--"

"Thanks, mom I'll see you after work then. I've got to get back." Jasmine hung up. She knew her mom would find it odd that she wanted to look at the room which just might be a crime scene.

Jasmine closed her laptop and nudged Francis with a toe. He stretched and gave a great big open-mouthed yawn. He stood up and with Jasmine sitting; they were just about face to face. She ran both hands over his face and he seemed to smile. She clipped his leash in place.

"Come on, you." She said to Francis and he was happy to cooperate. They went out to the dog yard in the back and Jasmine noticed a few extra cars parked in the alley. She and Francis stretched their legs and Claire came out to meet them.

"Thought I might find you two back here. Ready for lunch?" Claire asked brightly.

"I'm starved." Jasmine realized she had forgotten to eat her protein bar.

They walked through the alley and around the corner up to the Muffin Man Deli. They sat outside so Francis could laze in the sun. Jasmine looped his leash around the foot of her chair. She was still somewhat worried that he may be a runner. The crowd had thinned since morning; Jasmine guessed everyone must be off enjoying farm tours or shopping.

They ordered steamy bowls of tomato bisque and golden grilled provolone sandwiches. Though the food was definitely dressed up, this lunch took Jasmine right back to her childhood. She savored her soup and dipped a crisp corner of her sandwich before taking an unladylike bite.

Claire seemed to enjoy the simple lunch equally, they hardly spoke through lunch. Slow savored lunches were a rare gift in their lives since they'd opened their clinic. Claire finished her meal and sat back in her seat. Francis got up and scooped her hand up with his nose. She stroked the dog who seemed rather happy with himself.

"How's this sweet little dude doing as a roommate?" Claire inquired.

"He's doing well but he seems to think he's a person," Jasmine answered Claire raised an eyebrow and Jasmine continued. "He's forever on my furniture. I bought him his own bed and everything, but he insists on sleeping with me."

"Well, they do call it FURniture." Claire laughed. "But he's fully potty trained? No accidents? Doesn't eat your shoes?"

"Oh no, we've had no problems like that." Jasmine hadn't even considered that Francis might eat her beloved shoe collection.

"Then I'd say you're doing pretty great. I spoke to someone at Precious Paws rescue this morning. No one has called looking for him." Claire tipped forward and whispered something to Francis.

"It's so hard to believe no one is looking for him. I guess maybe he could have traveled further than we think." Jasmine wondered out loud.

"He could be from anywhere. His family could have been traveling with him. He could belong to a trucker who is thousands of miles away by now. It's a pity but dogs go missing every day." Claire continued to pet Francis and play with his floppy ears. He grinned and panted happily.

"True," Jasmine replied. "I won't be heartbroken if they don't turn up," she finished honestly.

"I know you won't." Claire continued, "Cause look at this face. Look at it!" The women laughed.

"Hey, will you take Francis back to the office? I've got to go see something with my mom." Jasmine passed the leash to Claire.

"Sure, we'll hang out. Everything okay?" Claire asked.

"Oh yeah, everything is okay. Call me if anything comes up."

"Okay." Claire and Francis headed back toward the alley while Jasmine crossed Grand Avenue and made her way to the historic Lyric Theatre. She noticed the all black police car parked in front, next to her mom's SUV.

Jasmine found the front door unlocked and, against her better judgment, she slipped inside. It was rather spooky without all the lights and staff. She took the hall around the great room of the theatre, back toward the set workshop and dressing rooms. She found Donna Cline and Detective Williams standing outside what had been Lily Day's dressing room. Jasmine could hear a camera snapping away within the room. Williams looked less than pleased to see her.

"Dr. Cline. The Mayor asked us to take down the crime scene tape; he didn't want to frighten the tourists during the Festival of Leaves. But you know we're still investigating." Williams said with a serious tone.

"Yes, Detective I'm sorry about that. It's just that I have some information that might be helpful in your investigation." Jasmine smiled, hopeful that Williams was finished scolding her.

"Information? What's that?" The Detective did seem to relax slightly.

"Well, I saw in the paper that they believe Lily suffocated." Jasmine began.

"That's right. Of course, we're still waiting for the official cause of death." Williams interrupted.

"Of course. But I was wondering how someone suffocates, alone in a dressing room. It seemed strange to me." Jasmine had the Detective's full attention now. "So I got to thinking about things that could cause sudden suffocation, like anaphylaxis. You know, your airways close up because of a chemical or allergen," she explained.

"You mean like from a bee sting, or peanuts or something?" Williams inquired.

“Exactly.” Jasmine nodded.

Williams flipped through a tiny notebook. “Hm she didn’t have an allergy to nuts or shellfish in her chart, the medical examiner mentioned that last night.”

“But she did have an equine allergy,” Jasmine interjected.

“Equine? As in horses?” Williams sounded unconvinced.

“Yes, horses, or their hair, saliva, or dander,” Jasmine answered. Williams considered this information for a moment.

“How do you know that Lily Day had an equine allergy?” The Detective inquired.

“She told me herself. I had been out to the Benton’s stables to see a pregnant mare. I wear coveralls when I go out to farms and Lily brushed by them hanging on the door in my office. Even in a gym bag, it made her sneeze profusely. She had to rush off and get some Benadryl.” Jasmine answered.

“I’m glad you brought this to me. Thank you.” Williams said frankly and glanced into the dressing room. A young man seemed to be finishing up his series of photos.

“Although I’m not sure there are many horses back here.” Williams thought out loud.

“Well, they make all kinds of things out of horsehair. Hairbrushes, makeup, and paintbrushes, too.” Donna offered.

“Oh, you’re right. I forgot about that; don’t wear a lot of makeup myself.” Williams made notes in her small notepad. The young man with the camera emerged.

"I got every angle possible. I promise." He said and headed straight past the ladies down the hall.

"Why would someone with a horse allergy use brushes made of horsehair?" Donna asked.

"They wouldn't." Jasmine and Detective Williams said, together. They exchanged a look.

"They would use acrylic brushes." Jasmine continued. "But, if someone knew about that allergy…" Jasmine trailed off.

"And had a motive," Williams added.

"They could have swapped out brushes." Jasmine finished.

Williams made more notes in her pad.

"Does this door lock?" Williams gestured to the door of the dressing room.

"Only from the inside," Donna replied.

"In that case, I'd like to keep everyone out of the building. Just until the morning. If you can stick around a while, I'd like to send someone to collect evidence from the dressing table." Williams said this and started down the hall. The Cline women followed.

"Didn't they collect evidence Saturday night?" Jasmine asked.

"Of course, but it's not customary to collect makeup brushes as evidence in a possible homicide," Williams said over her shoulder.

"Oh. Of course." Jasmine realized Williams was going to check out her lead.

"Naturally, the official story is still that there hasn't been a homicide." Williams turned at the door and gave them a stern look.

"Naturally." They replied in unison.

"Thanks, ladies, I'll be in touch." Williams was off. Donna turned on a few lights and plopped onto an ancient tufted sofa near the doors and Jasmine joined her.

"You think someone killed Lily with a makeup brush?" Donna asked with a huff.

"I'm not sure, mom. But I guess it's possible. Can you tell me what happened Saturday night?" Jasmine sat back and coughed. The old sofa was dusty, tiny particles of dust floated by in the dim lobby lights.

"Well. The show went off without a hitch. People milled around out here and had drinks; some of the actors came out and mingled. It was nice." Donna explained.

"Some of the actors? Lily?" Jasmine asked.

"Well, no. Sam was out here, though. Most of them were out here. You know actors, they love the attention." Donna shrugged.

"What happened after that? Anything strange?" Jasmine didn't enjoy grilling her mother but she just had to know what happened that fateful night.

"Well, after a while people headed home, including most of the cast and crew, and just as I was about to have Mark start locking things up, that's when I heard Vicki scream."

"She found Lily's body? Where was she?" Jasmine was full of questions.

"She was lying in front of her dressing table." Donna's face fell with the memory.

"Mom, if I promise not to touch anything, can you show me?" Jasmine asked.

"Well, they got all their pictures. I don't see any harm in taking a look. Come on."

They walked together back to the dressing room. When they reached it, Jasmine realized she had never been inside. She was surprised to see how drab it was. Lily had embodied the style and glamour of old Hollywood. This little room was not glamorous. The walls were unfinished like the hall, just studs and wood panels. There was a free-standing full-length mirror that looked as old as the theatre itself. Beside it was a small vanity with a trifold mirror that was framed with large old fashioned Christmas bulbs. The vanity table was covered with a lovely sateen scarf; bright patterns swirled inside an emerald border. There were similar scarves draped around the room as decor. Laid out on the scarf lay a vast makeup collection, including brushes in all sizes. There was a vintage looking vanity set right in the middle of everything. A matching comb, brush, and mirror. Their new Victorian scroll was meant to look aged, but they gleamed so brightly they must be brand new.

"These are lovely." Jasmine gestured to the set.

"Aren't they? Sam gave them to Lily Friday night. I think he ordered them from your friend Moira." Donna replied.

"An opening night gift? Did anyone mention that to Detective Williams?" Jasmine queried.

"Well, no. I guess I hadn't considered it." Donna said.

"Why would you? But what if -" Jasmine began.

"What if that brush is horse hair?" Donna finished.

“Exactly!” Jasmine exclaimed.

“I’ll let Detective Williams know right away.” Donna pulled out her phone.

“Okay. Let’s get out of here.” The room felt heavy and Jasmine was compelled to get out of it straight away. Maybe the room had been brighter with Lily in it.

The two women parted ways at the front door, Donna had to wait for an officer to come collect more evidence. Jasmine had another mission in mind. She wanted to go talk to Moira about the vanity set Sam had ordered for his wife.

Jasmine made her way slowly back up the street. There were people everywhere, stopped at the food trucks, carrying hot drinks and locally brewed ciders. Kids were running underfoot, to get a glimpse of the animals in a small petting zoo, or to ask their parents for money to buy caramel apples.

As she neared Blackbird, Jasmine realized her timing was no good. The store was packed. She caught sight of Moira under a huge pile of clothes, trying to ring people up and answer their questions at the same time. Jasmine shook her head and turned to go back to her own office. Her questions could wait.

Back at the office, everyone was milling around the front desk. Even Francis was lying across one of the vinyl benches where people waited with their pets.

“Working hard, I see.” Jasmine joked.

“Well, you can see the patients are just lined up around the block.” Claire laughed.

“It’s going to be a long week, boss.” Ellie chimed in.

“I think you’re right. But we got our wish, there actually IS a zoo out there.” Jasmine chuckled and gestured to the street.

“A zoo?” Ellie asked.

“A petting zoo. You guys should go check it out. No use standing around here.” Jasmine smiled.

“Okay!” Brian piped in. The younger staff all grabbed coats and hurried off.

“You’re not going to join them?” Claire leaned against the big desk.

“Nah, there will be plenty of time this week to see it all. Besides, if I go back out there, there’s no way I can walk by the mini-donuts again. What about you?” Jasmine asked.

“I think I’ll go catch a movie. You know how much I loooove crowds.” Claire was being sarcastic.

“Yeah? What’s playing?” Jasmine asked her old friend.

“I don’t even know, but this close to Halloween there’s bound to be something spooky playing.” Claire grinned.

“I’ll leave you to it.” Jasmine had no stomach for horror films. “I think Francis and I will go check out a new trail.”

“Have fun!” Claire slipped into her fall coat and out the front door. Jasmine locked up and went to gather her things. Just as she was locking up her phone vibrated in her pocket. She was juggling too many things between the dog and her bags and the keys to take a look at who was calling.

“Hello?” She answered in a pleasant tone.

“Hey, beautiful.” Eric’s soft husky voice greeted her.

"Oh Eric, hi." Jasmine sighed happily.

"Are you busy?" He asked.

"Not at all, it's dead here we're all kicking out early," Jasmine answered.

"Same here, all my clients are busy. I was just going to get away from the crowds with a hike." He hesitated and Jasmine heard him gulp a large breath. "I thought you might like to join me. What do you say?" Eric asked and Jasmine could swear he sounded nervous.

"I'd love to. Where?" She couldn't hesitate even if she'd wanted to play it cool.

"I'll text you the address; it's one of my favorite trails," Eric answered.

"Great, I'll see you in a few." Jasmine nearly squeaked after she hung up. What was it about Eric that made her feel like a schoolgirl?

She deposited her bags in the back and coaxed Francis into the Jeep. Her phone buzzed with a text from Eric. The address to the trailhead. She flipped down her visor to check her teeth in the mirror and remembered she hadn't worn makeup today. Oh well, he'd have to see her without makeup eventually, right? She smashed a few unruly curls back into place and turned the ignition.

The Laurentian Trail was just 15 miles northeast of town, straight up the highway. Jasmine remembered the place from her high school years but couldn't recall having hiked or run its trails. There was a convenient parking area and rest station just off the highway. She pulled in right next to Eric's truck and as she and Francis hopped out of the Jeep, she found him sitting on a picnic table. He had on sturdy hiking boots and dark denim jeans, a classic buffalo plaid flannel, and a black fleece vest. His blonde hair was unruly, waves crashing in every direction. He smiled broadly at her approach and reached out to give her a squeeze.

"Hi," was all he said.

"Hi," Jasmine repeated.

"You think our pal is up for the hike?" Eric nodded to Francis.

"Oh, I think he'll love it," Jasmine replied.

"The long way, or the short way?" Eric gestured to the two entrances into the woods behind him.

"Which is your favorite?" Jasmine asked.

"Well. The long way I guess." He tipped his chin to the northernmost entry.

"I'm game," Jasmine answered.

Together the three of them headed into the woods. Eric set a leisurely pace and Jasmine was pleased to find that Francis heeled beautifully. He sniffed things at the edge of the trail and took notice of squirrels and birds moving in the brambles, but he didn't tug or try to chase. He would probably make a great running partner.

The trail was lined with red and orange leaves, maple and oak trees were dappled throughout the pine forest. Jasmine saw mostly spruce and jack pine but noticed a few huge old white pines as well. She loved these woods. She breathed deeply, enjoying the scent of pine needles mixed with fresh fallen leaves, and maybe a hint of Eric's cedar cologne. She reached out and took his hand. Eric smiled.

"I have a confession to make," Eric said softly.

"Yeah? Should I be concerned?" Jasmine asked, teasing.

"No, I hope not. It's just that I had wanted to ask you out for a long time. I'm really glad you invited me to the play. I don't… I don't want you to feel like we're moving too fast." Eric finished. Jasmine heard nerves in his voice again.

"Oh, I wouldn't worry about that." She replied and squeezed his hand. She was pleased to see his smile return.

"Good. I haven't dated much since I started my practice." Eric admitted.

"Me either. I'm kind of rusty, to be honest." Jasmine said.

"Me too," Eric replied. He stopped walking and turned to her. "But I like spending time with you."

Jasmine felt herself flush. "I love spending time with you."

Eric bent to leave a small kiss on her cheek. He turned and they resumed their hike in the north woods.

"Any news on Lily Day? Do they still think her death was an accident?" Eric changed the topic suddenly.

"Well. I stumbled upon something. The Detective is going to check it out." Jasmine replied. She wasn't sure how much she should tell him

"You stumbled upon something? Like… evidence?" Eric queried, quite puzzled.

"Sort of? They haven't completed the autopsy but the preliminary cause of death is suffocation. I wondered how she might suffocate alone in a dressing room, you know? Then I remembered that Lily had an equine allergy." Jasmine explained.

"Wow. Those can be pretty serious." Eric paused to consider what Jasmine had said. "Wait, why is the detective checking that out?"

"Well. There are makeup and hairbrushes made of horsehair. Naturally, a girl with an allergy to horse hair wouldn't use them. Maybe she used one by mistake. But what if someone switched her brushes intentionally?" Jasmine didn't know who or why but she couldn't help but think that Sam must have a reason to believe his wife had been murdered. She suddenly had a strong desire to speak with Sam Day.

"I guess that is a possibility." Eric agreed.

The trail wound back around on itself and Jasmine realized they would soon return to the parking lot. The sun had vanished behind some ominous-looking clouds and the wind was picking up. Leaves swirled in wild patterns on the trail before them.

"Looks like rain," Eric noted. Jasmine nodded and wound her fingers around his arm.

"I wonder why anyone would want to kill Lily." Jasmine wondered aloud.

"Me too. But I guess everyone has secrets. Maybe there's something we don't know about her." Eric considered aloud.

"Or Sam." Jasmine finished.

They enjoyed the last yards of their walk in silence. Francis had slowed down, the walk was taking out of him. Jasmine knew he'd sleep well when they got home. As they approached their vehicles, she dug around in a pocket for her keys.

"The long route wasn't long enough today," Eric said so softly that Jasmine almost missed it over the wind. He bent to kiss her cheek. She stretched up on tiptoe to kiss him properly. She felt his lips smile again and she just loved that.

"Text me later?" She asked with a warm smile.

"Mhm." He answered with a nod. He looked a little breathless and not from their hike.

Jasmine turned and opened a door for Francis before hopping in the Jeep herself. The rain started as she drove home and Francis whined softly from the back seat. He mustn't like storms, Jasmine thought. Just as she parked in front of her small cottage, the rain started to pour down, accompanied by thunder and bursts of lightning. She left her things in the Jeep and together she and Francis made a mad dash for the front door.

Despite their run, Jasmine was soaked by the time she got inside. Poor Francis was soaked, too. She kicked off her boots and grabbed an old towel for Francis. She dried him gently. He nuzzled into her shoulder and neck and she gave him a small hug. She poured him some fresh water and stripped on her way to the bathroom. She ran a hot bath. The cold rain had chilled her to the bone.

Jasmine sank blissfully into the hot steaming water. She'd only left Eric's side a half-hour ago. It was silly to miss him, right? She chuckled to herself. She sunk deeper into the tub and let herself daydream about a life with Eric. She imagined a big farmhouse with a vast kitchen where they could cook together and entertain their friends. She could see them laughing and cooking together, surrounded by their family. Eric would care for the larger animals and she would look after the little ones. Little ones, huh. She hadn't even considered if Eric wanted a family.

A large crack of thunder shook her out of her daydream and Francis came charging into the room. For a second she thought he might jump into the bath with her.

"Down!" She scolded and he stopped just short of leaping into her bath. She stroked his head, poor thing was shaking like a leaf. She got up and slid her arms into an oversized bathrobe. Her dark hair fell in damp ringlets over the lush cream terrycloth.

“Come on, you.” She called to Francis. He followed as she went to the kitchen and poured herself a glass of wine. She poured some kibble into his dish. This time he wasn’t interested in the kibble. Jasmine sighed. Some dogs just hated thunder.

She lit a few candles and pulled out a big throw blanket from a basket near the couch. She curled up and draped the blanket across the sofa.

“Okay. I give up. Come here.” Jasmine said and patted the seat next to her. Francis didn’t hesitate. He leaped onto the couch and curled up with his head on her hip. She stroked his head, soothing him. He seemed to calm.

Jasmine flipped on the TV and she and Francis enjoyed a quiet night in. He wasn’t a handsome veterinarian, but Francis was a decent date on a rainy autumn evening.

CHAPTER SEVEN

Jasmine woke with a start. She felt disoriented until she realized it was because her phone was ringing. Just as she lifted it from her nightstand, it stopped. She flopped back into her pillows while it went to voicemail. A few moments later, it buzzed so she picked it up and pressed play.

"Good morning Dr. Cline, this is Detective Williams. Sorry to wake you so early but I wanted to let you know that you may be onto something with the equine allergy. The medical examiner says that Mrs. Day had severe angioedema along her scalp and neck, which indicates an allergic response. I also found that Mrs. Day had a standing prescription for an epi-pen, but none could be located in her personal effects. I wanted to thank you for the tip, I'll stop by your shop later today."

That was good news. Jasmine was pleased to hear she had perhaps been helpful in the mysterious Lily Day case. She was less than pleased to see that it was 5:30 am. She sighed and rolled over, hoping for a little more sleep. Jasmine found herself face to face with Francis, who was lying on the bed with his face on the pillow like a human.

"Good grief." She muttered. She got out of bed. Francis hopped out with her and they wandered together to the back door. She clipped his leash on and they stepped outside. It was still dark out and though it had stopped raining, there were low rumbles of thunder in the distance. Francis spent no time dallying and they were back in the kitchen in a flash. Jasmine started a pot of coffee, she would surely need it today.

Jasmine got into her running gear. She switched her usual running shoes for some designed for gravel trails. She thought she may need the extra grip on a trail covered in wet leaves. She slipped on a rain jacket and left Francis behind on the three-seasons porch.

The wind had already picked up. Jasmine zipped her jacket and stretched. She chose some fast-paced house music for her run and hit the trail. Before six am on a rainy day, Jasmine had the trail to herself. She picked up pace fast, the cold was an excellent motivator. Before she knew it, Jasmine was ready to turn back. She paused to look out over the valley. Fortunately, the leaves hadn't been wiped out by the storm. With the coming dawn, she could see thunderheads in the distance. She turned to head home and saw someone in a dark rain poncho coming down that side trail in a dark rain poncho.

As she approached the stranger she realized it was Vicki Adams again. Jasmine smiled in greeting but Vicki avoided eye contact as they passed each other. Jasmine could see the other young woman's shoulders heaving. That was a tough trail, she'd have to try it out later this week, but not in this rain.

She got home and took off her rain jacket. Francis licked her hand to say hello. She patted his head and poured some dog food into his dish. While she was frustrated about his sleeping habits, she had to admit it was nice to have his company. She poured herself a big cup of coffee and headed to the bedroom. She sat next to the nightstand to check her phone.

She had a couple of emails but she decided to read those at work, well after her coffee had kicked in. She typed out a cheery good morning for Eric. She chose a jazz playlist and set the phone in a speaker cradle.

Jasmine got ready to her custom playlist. Something about the jazz and rain settled her mood. She was a creature of habit, waking up to calls from detectives could have thrown off her whole day. She decided not to let that happen.

Today she chose a deep rose sweater and dark denim jeans. She smoothed on lipstick that matched her sweater and since it was rainy, some waterproof mascara. The rain also meant her curls would be impossible to manage, so she applied some gel and took the time to French braid it, leaving a few ringlets out to frame her face. Francis wandered into her room as she was choosing a coat for the day. She settled on black leather.

They arrived at work before everyone, even Ellie. Jasmine went around and turned on all the lights. She glanced outside and the gloom lent a very Halloween look to the Festival of Leaves decorations. Despite the weather, there were a few people out setting up food trucks and vendor booths.

Jasmine turned on the computer at the front desk and was disappointed to find she had no appointments set for the day.

“What on earth are we going to do today, huh?” She asked Francis. The front door jingled. “Mornin’ Ellie!” Jasmine called from behind the desk. Ellie gasped, startled before she broke into laughter.

“Jeez, you scared me. What are you doing here so early?” Ellie asked.

“Got an early start today. Though, if I’d checked the schedule yesterday, I might have just gone back to bed.”

“There’s only one appointment all day. Maybe I should have mentioned that. Sorry.” Ellie set down her bags and hung her damp coat up on a hook in the hall.

“Oh, that’s okay. Does Claire only have one appointment? Wow. Maybe next year we’ll close for the festival.” Jasmine got up so Ellie could have her usual seat.

“Maybe we should.” Ellie agreed.

Jasmine puttered around the office for a couple of hours. She did an inventory of supplies and put in a few orders for things they were short on. She dusted bottles of medication and shelves full of gauze packets. When she was satisfied that everything was clean and in order, it was only 9:30 am. She plopped into her office chair, frustrated. She was not good at having nothing to do.

She opened her laptop and found the browser still open to that article about Lily Day. She closed the tab and sat back in her chair. Why did Sam insist that Lily’s death had been intentional, rather than a tragic accident? She opened their patient management application. She typed in Day in the search bar, and there was the Day’s Home address. She jotted it down on a post-it note and closed the laptop.

“Hang out here for a while, okay?” She said to Francis and grabbed her coat. She slipped out the back door unnoticed. The Days lived just five minutes away, near Merritt Valley elementary school. Jasmine found their house easily and as she pulled in front of it to park across the street, she saw a slight figure in a dark rain jacket run up to the front door. The figure dropped a note into the mail slot and then, rather than come back out to the sidewalk, they ran around the side of the house and out of sight.

Jasmine shut off her Jeep and walked up to the front door. She paused… what on earth was she going to say to Sam Day? ‘Hey, how are you? Why do you think Lily was murdered? Okay, good talk!’ She shook her head. She was about to turn around and get back in her Jeep when Sam opened the door.

“Dr. Cline? Wha… what are you doing here?” Sam asked in confusion. He was still in plaid pajama pants and a white t-shirt. His red hair was a mess and he hadn’t shaved in a couple of days.

Jasmine cleared her throat. “I - I just wanted to talk to you, Sam. I was so sorry to hear about Lily.” She said sincerely.

“Thanks. Me too.” Sam’s eyes fell to the floor. He bent to pick up the envelope. “Oh were you just leaving this card?” He tore open the small square envelope.

“No, but I saw someone drop it off as I arrived. I can go if it’s a bad time.” She answered awkwardly.

“No no, come on in. Sorry for the mess, I haven’t been off the couch much.” Sam wandered into the house and Jasmine followed. Daisy barked and hopped down from a wingback chair near a window. Jasmine bent to pat her head.

“She keeps looking for Lil,” Sam said wistfully. “Please, have a seat. I’d offer you something but there’s not much in the fridge. He sat back down on the couch. The house itself was tidy and cozy, furnished in Lily’s old Hollywood style. The area around the couch, however, was littered with pizza boxes and empty cans. Jasmine chose a chair opposite the couch.

“Sam, I’m so sorry to bother you. But I’ve spoken to Detective Williams.” Jasmine began.

“And she thinks Lily’s death was an accident.” Sam interrupted.

“Well, yes. But you believe she was murdered?” Jasmine just spat it out.

“I know she was,” Sam answered, firmly.

“I’m inclined to believe you.” Jasmine’s response surprised Sam. “But I wanted to know what makes you think that.”

“These damn letters.” Sam motioned to a small pile of already opened envelopes. “I started to get them a few weeks ago. First, they just seemed like harmless fan mail. I know we’re not famous but both Lily and I have been in a couple of bigger shows and sometimes real theatre geeks will get crazy about one actor.” Sam suddenly remembered the envelope in his hand. He pulled a sympathy card out and opened it.

“So you think this fanatic writing Lily letters may have hurt her?” Jasmine asked.

Sam was distracted by the letter. He mumbled some curses under his breath.

“That’s the thing, Dr. Cline. The letters were written to me. Look.” He passed the card across the table.

It read; “I’m sorry about your wife. It just wasn’t meant to be. Now I think you will find, you’ve got time for me.” It was signed simply; Always, yours.

“Oh, wow. This letter is creepy, Sam. Do they all rhyme?” Jasmine asked.

Sam nodded as he reached over and took the card back.

“This is the one I got Saturday night.” Sam flipped through the pile and passed her a card in a bright red envelope. A simple white card inside was scrolled in the same neat handwriting.

“Your wife must go. Her time has passed. Soon you’ll know a love that lasts.” This time it wasn’t signed.

“Oh Sam, does Detective Williams know about these?” Jasmine didn’t slip the note back into its envelope before setting it on the coffee table.

“No. They didn’t want to hear from me, they insisted Lily’s death was an accident. She is supposed to stop here today, though. Oh god, I guess I should get cleaned up.” Sam stood and started to collect pizza boxes. He rushed out of the room with a pile of trash. Jasmine swiftly pulled out her phone and snapped a picture of the note.

Sam returned just as she was putting her phone back in her pocket.

“Well, I better get going. Sam, do you mind if I drop off some things for you tomorrow? Maybe some food that doesn’t come from a cardboard box?” Jasmine asked and she made her way toward the front door.

“You know, that would be nice. Thanks for stopping by, Doc.” Sam saw her to the door. As he closed it behind her, Jasmine pulled out her phone to make sure she’d caught that picture. She had. She thought she’d let the Detective have her meeting with Sam before she brought this to her. Besides, Jasmine had another mission in mind.

Jasmine pulled into the back parking lot at Merritt Valley Mobile Animal Clinic just after 11 am. She took the alley through between buildings and walked into Blackbird, the local clothing boutique less than 5 minutes later. Several women were browsing but it was nothing like the mob Jasmine had seen in the shop yesterday.

The shop's owner, Moira, was sitting on the front counter, chatting with a young woman about sizes. Moira was fair-skinned with raven hair, currently cut in an asymmetrical bob with blunt bangs. Under the black, there were pockets of bright purple that shone through as Moira moved. Today she was wearing a black A-line dress with red cherries printed all over it. She was wearing red peep-toe shoes and a huge red petticoat. She was surrounded by its endless ruffles and Jasmine guessed she might have taken that perch on the counter to show them off.

"Hey, Jazz!" Moira called. "Need another dress already? Date number 2?" She grinned.

"Actually I came to see you about something else, though I think we've already had dates number 2 and 3." Jasmine smiled up at her old friend.

"TWO more dates already? Why it hasn't even been a week!" Moira hopped down off the counter. "So what can I do for you, babe?"

"I have a question for you." Jasmine peered around the store at the women shopping. "You think we could talk somewhere more private? Just for a second."

"Sure. Let me show you to my office." Moira walked back toward the dressing rooms and motioned for Jasmine to follow. She opened a bright teal door at the end of that hall. She sat in an oversized tufted chair behind a desk strewn with catalogs and stacks of paper. Jasmine closed the door behind them.

"Sorry to take you from your customers, I promise to be brief."

"It's okay, the longer they browse the more they'll find," Moira said with a wink. "What is it, Jazz? Is everything okay?"

"Did Sam Day order a gift set from you? For his wife?" Jasmine inquired.

"Oh yeah, he did. A couple of weeks ago. She had this whole movie star thing going on, you saw the dressing gowns. He wanted to get her a vanity set like those old Hollywood stars used." Moira picked through a pile of wholesale catalogs and chose one. She flipped through it and held it out for Jasmine to see. Of course, it was the same set that had been on Lily's vanity table in her dressing room at the Lyric theatre.

"It came in last week. How come?" Moira adjusted her glasses.

"I - I'm just curious about something. I promise I'll explain later. Is that brush made of horsehair as antique brushes would have been?" Jasmine asked.

"No. Huh Sam was specific that it couldn't be horsehair. That's why he came to me instead of ordering online." Moira passed the catalog to Jasmine and pointed to the description. "See, the brush is 100% acrylic". Jasmine read it for herself and set the book aside.

"Hm. That is interesting." Jasmine stood up to go.

"Hey wait, are you going to tell me what's going on?" Moira stood too.

"Oh, I promise I will. Over dinner? I'm free so much this week, the Festival of Leaves has the opposite effect on our business." Jasmine said as she opened the bright door.

"Dinner would be nice. My place, tonight? I haven't cooked for you in ages." Moira offered. They made their way down the hall.

"Oh, I'd love that!" Jasmine replied.

"Great. 7 pm? That is if you haven't got a date already," Moira teased.

Jasmine laughed, "No I don't, not tonight."

“Well, I want to hear all about dates one through three. In detail! See you tonight.” Moira’s customers were starting to circle so Jasmine slipped out of the shop. Dinner with Moira sounded wonderful, she was a great cook and they hadn’t spent much time together since Jasmine had moved back to town.

Jasmine made her way back to the office. She passed several food trucks on the way and stopped to get herself a big slice of pizza. She was munching on it as she got into the office.

“Mm, that looks good!” Ellie said over a pile of textbooks.

“Mhm,” Jasmine answered, her mouth full.

“The Humane Society called. They said that no one had reported any large tan bully mixes missing and they’ve only had one call since he was on TV this weekend.” Ellie passed over her note about the call.

“What did they say about the one call they’ve had?” Jasmine asked.

“It was a man who claimed his neighbor had a dog like that, and he hadn’t seen the dog or his neighbor in a couple of weeks.”

“Oh. Did they say where that man was from?”

Ellie set her face in a hand and gazed off in the distance as if looking for the answer. “Oh yeah, they said he was from Gilbert.” She finally replied.

“That’s almost 30 miles away. I wonder if Francis ran that far.” Jasmine mused out loud. She suddenly realized Francis would need to go out. “Thanks, Ellie!” She called over her shoulder.

Jasmine’s worries over Francis faded immediately, she found the dog stretched out relaxing in her office. He lifted his head to look at her as she entered and his tail thumped in rhythm as his it began to wag.

She sat and finished her pizza. She snuck Francis a small piece of crust.

"Did you miss me?" Jasmine thought for a moment. "I wonder if someone else is out there missing you." She gazed into the dog's gentle, sweet brown eyes. He rested his head on her knee and she stroked his head for a few minutes.

"C'mon let's go outside," she said and clipped his leash into place. As the pair got out to the small dog yard behind their building, a big black police vehicle pulled up next to Jasmine's Jeep. Detective Williams had mentioned she would stop by today.

"Afternoon Dr. Cline," Williams said as she exited her SUV.

"Jasmine, please. Good afternoon Detective." Jasmine nodded hello.

"Nice looking dog." Williams complimented Francis. "I wonder if you have a few minutes to talk?"

"Sure." Jasmine agreed and Williams followed her to her office. Jasmine offered the detective a seat but she preferred to stand. Jasmine rested against her desk.

"I've just come from speaking with Sam Day. I understand you were there earlier this morning?" Williams seemed to want confirmation, though she obviously knew the answer to her question.

"That's right," Jasmine answered.

"What business did you have with Sam Day this morning?" Williams asked seriously.

"I wanted to give him my condolences." Jasmine thought it best to leave out her curiosity about the circumstances surrounding Lily Day's death.

"Mm. Of course." Williams took a seat after all and Jasmine followed suit, sitting in her desk chair.

"I suppose Sam might have mentioned the letters he received in the weeks leading up to his wife's death?" Williams asked.

"He did. Actually, I saw someone in a dark rain poncho drop one off as I arrived at his house." Jasmine divulged.

Williams got out her notepad. "You did? Can you describe them for me?"

"Well, I only saw them from the back, and as I said they had on a raincoat. The hood was up so I didn't see their face. I would say they were small build though, maybe 5'4" or 5'5"."

"Probably a woman, then," Williams thought aloud.

"I'm sorry, Detective. Was there something I can help you with?" Jasmine wanted to get to the point.

"I'm not sure yet. You seem to have some insight and connection to this case. I don't know what to think about that yet." Williams mentioned frankly. Jasmine wasn't sure she liked the Detective's tone.

"Okay?" Jasmine said curiously.

"Dr. Cline, were you planning to tell me about the threatening notes Sam received before his wife's suspicious death?" Williams inquired.

"Yes. In your message this morning you said you'd stop by my office today, and here you are. I thought we'd discuss it then. I took a photo of one for that purpose." Jasmine produced her phone and showed the young Detective the photo of the threatening note.

"Though, since you've now seen the letters yourself I'm not sure it matters how you learned about them." Jasmine sat back and set her phone down, crossing her arms.

"Fair point," Williams said and made some notes. "We've collected the notes as evidence. Thanks to you, and that last note you've got a picture of, this case has officially been upgraded to a homicide investigation."

CHAPTER EIGHT

Jasmine rushed home, it was nearly 6 pm. She didn't know how she'd lost so much time since she'd had no appointments all afternoon. She supposed she had lost almost 2 hours talking with Detective Williams. At times their talk had felt more like an interrogation. More than once, Williams had hinted that Jasmine might have ulterior motives.

Then, of course, Jasmine had to catch the entire staff up on her conversation with the Detective. You don't just have a police officer in your office for a couple of hours without raising some eyebrows. Claire was particularly interested in Williams and her intentions.

By the time Jasmine had left the office, she was at risk of being late for her dinner with Moira Randall. Jasmine was never late for anything, and certainly not dinner with a dear friend.

She plunked down her things and hung up Francis's leash with her leather jacket. She nearly sprinted to the bedroom and stripped off her work clothes. She tossed them in the general direction of the hamper and stared into her closet. Dinner with the owner of a clothing boutique called for some real style. Her eyes settled on a full-length black dress with long sleeves and an elaborate cut out down the back. She freshened up and slid the long dress over her well-muscled curves. The dress was clingy and as Jasmine gazed into her full-length mirrors, she was glad that all the season's pastries hadn't made an appearance on her thighs.

She clasped on a long dramatic gold necklace. The chain was substantial and the pendant was an oversized black jewel with a full tassel made of the same thick chain. Jasmine sat at her dressing table. Her mind wandered briefly to poor Lily day who had died while sitting at her dressing table just as Jasmine was now.

Jasmine shook her head to clear the thought of it. She delicately unbraided her hair. Thanks to the French braid she'd worn all day, her lush curls fell in huge soft waves down around her shoulders. She spritzed on some shine spray to help keep it shining and smooth. She applied some high shine lipstick in a deep crimson. Tonight she even took the time to wing her eyeliner. When she was satisfied with her look she checked the time. It was 6:45 pm. She stepped into some black flats and hurried to the kitchen where she retrieved a bottle of red wine. She patted Francis's head and asked him to go to the porch. He obliged and it was exactly 6:50 pm when Jasmine threw her leather jacket over her dress and locked her front door.

Fortunately, Moira Randall lived only a few moments away on Lake Drive. This neighborhood was younger and trendier than Jasmine's quiet street. The massive brick homes on Majestic Lake were appealing to young couples and families who had moved to Merritt Valley from bigger cities for a taste of small-town Midwest life. Moira had inherited her parents' home here on the lake. It was an impressive house, with at least 5 bedrooms and several baths. As Jasmine came to a stop in the parking bay, she wondered if perhaps Moira was lonely in such a large house all alone.

Moira greeted Jasmine warmly at the door. "Oh, honey I'm so glad you came. You dressed for the occasion!" Moira beamed. Jasmine passed her the bottle of wine.

"Of course I did. Sorry, I wasn't sure what you're making, I hope red is okay." She said and shrugged out of her coat.

"Red is perfect. Oh, Merlot!" Moira took a closer look at the bottle. "You picked exactly the right wine. I made pasta and chicken Picante." She glanced up at Jasmine and motioned to the coat rack beside the door. "You chose the perfect dress, too. You should wear that on date 4." She said with a devilish laugh

Moira led her through the house to the dining room. Jasmine had forgotten how stately Moira's home was. The style of the house itself didn't suit Moira's funky eclectic persona, but the art on the walls and all the hand-chosen pieces of wildly colored furniture definitely did.

The formal dining room held the same traditional dining table Jasmine remembered from dinners at the Randalls' as a girl, but Moira had dry bushed its detailed scrollwork with a deep green and hues of blue. The chairs had been recovered with a brilliant pattern in the same shades. The chandelier had been updated to an artistic piece that Jasmine swore had to be one of a kind. Blown glass imitated long tropical stems, and the light bulbs were hidden within huge glass flowers.

Moira was pouring wine into glasses on a sideboard. The table was already set for two and enticing dishes of steaming food were displayed between the two place settings. Moira passed Jasmine a glass and gestured for her to sit.

"Wow Moira, that light fixture is amazing." Jasmine was trying not to gape as she sat down.

"Oh, I dated a glassblower for a while a few years ago." Moira smiled. "He's got a gallery in the city now." Moira had been married and divorced early on, while Jasmine was still in graduate school. She always seemed to have interesting boyfriends from all over the world since.

"Well, he was very talented," Jasmine said sincerely.

"He *certainly* was," Moira winked. The two women laughed and Moira took a sip of her wine. She served Jasmine a pile of pasta and placed a piece of the chicken on top of it.

"Now, tell me about this guy," Moira said, helping herself to the pasta.

"Well I mean, you know Eric." Jasmine took a bite of the pasta. She closed her eyes and savored the flavors. She'd forgotten how great a cook Moira was.

"Well, sure. But I don't know him well, and not nearly as well as you do." Moira took a bite herself.

“Oh. Goodness.” Jasmine side and took a generous drink from her wine glass. “Eric is so handsome. I’d always known that but spending so much time with him... He looks like the leading man in rom-com.” He really did. Tall, broad shoulders, lean and muscular. Tousled golden hair, enchanting deep blue eyes, full lips… strong jaw… Jasmine forgot where she was and blushed.

Moira giggled. “He is hot. But I knew that already. Everyone who sees the dude walking around town knows that, Jazz. What’s he like?”

“Confident. Kind. Funny?” Jasmine took a bite and chewed slowly, both enjoying the food and giving herself time to think. “The best thing though? He doesn’t play games. He didn’t wait 2 days to call me after our first date. He doesn’t wait to text me back. He sends me cute good mornings.”

“Oh, he got you with the good morning text, huh?” Moira teased. “I know you went to see the play Friday, tell me about these other two dates? Come to think of it I don’t know much about the play either. Tell me everything. ” Jasmine could tell Moira was genuinely interested to know what was going on in her life. Perhaps she hadn’t been on a date in a while so she was living vicariously through her friend, but Jasmine decided to indulge her.

“Well the night of the play was like a date, date, you know? He opened my doors and held my hand through rooms. God everyone at Taste of Rome noticed us when we walked in. At least that’s how it felt.” Jasmine felt flush.

“In that blue dress, I’m sure they did. Did he wear a suit?” Moira sipped her wine.

“He did. He knows how to wear one, too. The night was formal, but at the same time it was easy.” Jasmine set her fork down.

“Easy? How do you mean?”

“There weren’t awkward moments. No weird silences, I didn’t have to force a laugh at any of his jokes I never had to pretend to be interested while he talked about his work. It just felt natural to be together.” Jasmine finished.

"Oh babe, are you in trouble." Moira sounded serious but she was smiling. "Go on. Was there a kiss?"

"Was there ever," Jasmine replied and her old friend laughed.

"So how did you manage two more dates since Friday? It's only Tuesday." Moira quipped.

"Well, you know about Lily Day. After I found out, I was feeling upset about it and I sent Eric a text. He was feeling down, too, so he came over to keep me company." Jasmine poked around at the remains of her meal and decided she couldn't manage another bite. She lifted her wine glass and settled back into her seat.

"Kept you company, huh? And what did you two do together?" Moira's tone was suggestive and it made Jasmine laugh.

"Oh stop. We just watched old movies. Ate junk food. Cuddled on the couch." Jasmine remembered the evening fondly.

"So your second date was what most people do with their boyfriends on a Sunday? He didn't even make you watch football?" Moira cocked a perfectly groomed eyebrow.

"He certainly did not." Jasmine laughed, though, she'd probably watch football if it meant spending another evening on a couch with Eric. She might even pay attention.

"So, formal date, boyfriend date, what did you do on your third date? Plan the wedding?" Moira teased and the women laughed together.

"You're so silly. We went out and hiked Laurentian. Right before the storm yesterday." Jasmine was still smiling. Moira picked up plates and set them aside on the buffet. She poured them each a bit more wine.

"That sounds like an adventure and right up your alley. Honestly Jazz, all jokes aside I'm happy for both of you. I've wondered for a long time when you guys would hook up."

"Why does everyone keep saying that?" Jasmine called after Moira who vanished into the kitchen. She appeared with two slices of cheesecake, drizzled with some dark berry sauce. She set one plate in front of Jasmine and plopped back down with her own.

"Because you two are made for each other," Moira said frankly, scooping up a forkful of cheesecake.

Jasmine considered that while she took a bite of cheesecake, too. She made a pleasant sound with the decadent dessert in her mouth and Moira smiled brightly.

"You made this?" Jasmine asked, astounded.

"Mhm." Moira positively beamed.

"Wow. You could put Taste of Rome out of business. What is that sauce?" Jasmine took another bite. She didn't care if she had to run twice tomorrow.

"It's chokecherry syrup. I made that, too." Moira answered proudly.

"It's just divine. I've never tasted anything like it. How come you aren't a chef someplace?"

"Because I love to cook. I don't want it to be a job." Moira said with a matter-of-fact tone. "Speaking of jobs, what was that about at the shop today?"

“Oh, I nearly forgot.” Jasmine set her fork down. “They assumed Lily Day’s death was accidental. I remembered that she had an equine allergy and I mentioned that to the Detective on her case. I thought maybe a makeup brush or something. It turns out that she had a terrible rash on her scalp which indicates an allergic reaction. I saw her vanity set in her dressing room the other day. I guess I wondered if maybe Sam--”

“If Sam had ordered her a horse hairbrush.” Moira finished Jasmine’s train of thought.

“Exactly. Since it wasn’t horsehair, I’m not sure if it’s related. But they did upgrade her case to a homicide investigation today.” Jasmine took a breath and finished her dessert. She sat back, stuffed, and let out a contented sigh.

“How come?” Moira queried.

“Well, Sam had been receiving these suspicious letters for a while before Lily was killed. He got one Saturday night that threatened Lily’s life. Come to think of it, I have a picture of it.” Jasmine took out her phone and flipped to the photo. She passed her phone over to show her friend.

“Oh wow… You know Jazz, I’m not sure I should ask why you have a photo of that note.” Moira handed the phone back.

“Something about the whole thing just doesn’t sit right with me. I snapped the photo because I wasn’t sure Sam was going to show the Detective on the case. She’s not the warmest person to talk to.” Jasmine was still a little unsettled by Detective Williams’ attitude that afternoon.

“Well, no. I guess most police detectives probably aren’t.” Moira started to collect plates. Jasmine got up to help. “No, no, I’ll get this later. Come sit with me in the den for a bit. We’ll have some coffee.” Jasmine nodded, though she could not fathom eating or drinking another thing. She followed Moira through a dimly lit hall to her den. Jasmine had remembered this room full of leather-bound books, cigar boxes, and stuffed ducks. The books remained but the ducks had been replaced with stylized faux taxidermy sculptures in Moira’s signature bold jewel tones. The room was full of potted trees and hanging plants. It was more inviting this way, Jasmine thought.

Moira put on some soft music. She must have coffee here most mornings because there was a coffee bar near the door. Jasmine sat on a big leather couch and watched as Moira vanished to fetch water. She got some coffee going and came to sit near Jasmine.

"I'm so glad you came tonight. I feel like we never see each other. We should do this more often." Moira gave her shoulder a squeeze.

"We really should. My house, next time. I'm no chef but I can make a few things." Jasmine chuckled.

"Oh, I'm sure you can cook. I could give you some lessons, too. Seems like you might be cooking for someone else soon, too." Moira nudged her.

"I'd love lessons." Jasmine meant that. Moira fetched them small cups of coffee.

"What about you? I feel like we talked about me all night. Are you seeing anyone?" Jasmine blew on the piping hot coffee.

"Oh, no. I'm taking some time to focus on myself. I need time after Paulo." Moira said with a sigh. She seemed to sink into the couch.

"Paulo? He was the Portuguese singer, right?" Jasmine could hardly remember.

"Drummer." Moira corrected. "I think he broke my heart."

"What happened there?" Jasmine sipped her coffee.

"He stayed with me all last winter. His band had broken up and he was sort of, lost looking for direction. Then, he got an audition for some big artist's band and that was it." Moira sighed.

“He just left?” Jasmine asked rhetorically. “That’s awful.”

“Mhm. And the worst of it is he told me he still loves me, he just has to follow the music.”

“Well, I’m sure the right guy will come along when you’re ready.” Jasmine was reminded of her friend’s dramatic romantic life and while it sounded glamorous she didn’t envy it. She leaned forward and set her cup down.

“I know you’re right.” Moira sighed again. “I thought he was the right one. But, c’est la vie.”

Jasmine noticed the time, it was getting quite late. “I suppose I better get going.” She cleared her throat and stood up. “Before I fall into a food coma on your sofa.”

“Oh, I’ll walk you out.” They made their way through the old house and Moira fetched Jasmine’s leather coat for her. “This is a very stylish choice,” she mentioned as Jasmine shrugged into it.

“Thank you, I learned from the best. Oh thanks for dinner, this was wonderful.” Jasmine embraced her friend and reached for the door.

“My pleasure, I mean it, let’s do this again soon!” Moira waved and closed the door.

A few stars were peeking out in the night sky. Still a bit damp and chilly, but perhaps the clouds were clearing. When Jasmine got home she took Francis out and admired those stars while he sniffed about. She tidied up her mess from hurrying about before dinner and switched out her dress for cozy flannel pj’s. Francis didn’t even pretend he was going to sleep on the floor tonight, he was already on her bed when Jasmine finished brushing her teeth.

"Oh well." She said softly. She sank into the pillows. It had been a long full day. Between the wine and the rich food, Jasmine didn't have much time to replay the day's events. Although, one thing Moira said to her replayed across her thoughts. When speaking of herself and Eric, Moira had said, "The two of you were made for each other."

Jasmine drifted off pondering that idea.

Morning came and today Jasmine's whole routine would be thrown off. She knew she didn't have any appointments so she didn't intend to go to the office. Instead, Jasmine planned to make a large casserole for Sam Day and drop it off at his house. All other things aside Sam had no family in town and he had just lost his wife. In Jasmine's family, when people lost loved ones, you cooked for them.

She slid out of bed and smoothed out her side. Francis hopped down from his side and tugged at the corner of the comforter which made Jasmine laugh. Maybe it wouldn't be so bad if he learned to help make the bed. She didn't bother changing out of her PJs. She flipped through her phone as she wandered to the kitchen. Her mother wanted to meet for coffee later. Jasmine typed out a quick, "Sounds good," in response. She also had a message from Eric. It was a cartoon sun waving, with, "good morning sunshine!" written across it in bold print. Jasmine grinned. Jasmine smiled. She found a similar sunny emoji and wrote him a good morning in return. Francis whined at the back door.

"Oh I'm sorry, let's go," Jasmine said to the dog and grabbed his leash. They went for a short walk up the trail at the edge of the backyard. The weather could not make up its mind. It was cloudy and threatening rain again.

When she got back to the kitchen Jasmine put on some upbeat music. She filled Francis' dishes. She dug around in the cupboard for a disposable metal casserole pan. She mixed the ingredients without a recipe and in no time, her casserole was in the oven. She set a timer for 45 minutes and plunked down on the couch.

Francis flopped in front of her and she turned on the tv. The local news was covering the Festival of Leaves. They showed footage of the farm tours, which were wildly popular with tourists who'd never been to farm country. She caught a glimpse of her favorite large animal vet running a gloved hand over a huge red and white Holstein. He smiled at the camera.

Hayrides would begin today and several shuttles were running out to the orchards. Jasmine thought that might be fun. The news was surprisingly quiet on the matter of Merritt's first murder investigation in a century. She supposed the mayor had asked the Police Department to keep it quiet to avoid scaring off the tourists. the Festival of Leaves was supposed to be good old fashioned wholesome family fun.

Jasmine started some coffee and hopped in the shower. She smoothed her hair back in a braid again today and put on come brushed leggings and fitted black sweater over her tank top. She thought she'd play up the leather jacket, so she put on knee high black leather riding boots. By the time she'd put on some berry lipstick and quick mascara, she could hear the timer going off in the kitchen.

Jasmine sipped her coffee while the casserole cooled enough for transport. She nibbled some toast with plum jam one of her patients had brought in a few weeks ago. All the homemade food was one of Jasmine's favorite perks about moving home. These occasional lazy mornings were on that list as too. In the city, there was no such thing as a slow day.

She put the casserole in a soft-sided cooler, She asked Francis to go hang out in the back porch and had a thought. She ran to her room and grabbed his new fleece dog bed. She laid it in front of the long line of windows in the porch. Francis sniffed it and curled up on it immediately. At least it would get some use out here.

Jasmine and her casserole arrived at the Day household just before 10 am. She knocked and Sam greeted her. He looked more himself today, clean-shaven and hair combed. She followed Sam into the kitchen. She placed the family-sized casserole on the counter.

"Oh wow," Sam said. "That thing is huge. I mean… thank you."

"It will keep up to a week in the fridge and microwaves up nice." Jasmine knew it was probably too much but it was easy hearty comfort food.

"I appreciate it." Sam sounded sincere. "Did you hear they're finally investigating Lily's death?"

"I did. Detective Williams stopped to chat with me right after she left here yesterday. Do they have any suspects?" Jasmine inquired.

Sam poured two cups of coffee and offered one to Jasmine. "You mean besides me?" he said wryly. "No, I don't think so. I know it's just procedure but it seems silly to investigate me. I mean it took them four days for me to convince them she may have been murdered. Why would I do that, if I killed her?" Sam sounded cynical but Jasmine couldn't blame him.

"It doesn't make much sense." She agreed. "Do you have any ideas?"

"I just know it has to be someone in the cast. Or crew, I guess." Sam sipped his coffee.

"Why do you say that?" Jasmine implored.

"Three of those notes appeared at the theatre during closed rehearsals. The last one appeared five minutes before curtain call. The stage crew is strict about keeping audience members out of the backstage area." Sam explained.

"My mom has mentioned that. With all the lights and sets, and the pulleys for the curtains, people can get hurt. It's a liability." Jasmine added.

"Exactly. And all the volunteer staff in uniforms during performances - it's really hard for anyone else to get back there. They'd have to be a member of the show." Sam was convincing.

"So, do you have any ideas about who? Anyone who acted strangely on set?" Jasmine pried.

"Honestly. No. I mean, it's theatre. Everyone involved has their quirks." Sam had a point. Jasmine had known her share of theatre people and while she didn't like to stereotype, it took a certain flair to make it in that world.

"I guess you're right. I'll ask my mom what she thinks, since she was in the house for most of your rehearsals, maybe she noticed something." Jasmine offered and set down her cup. "Well, I better be off. I-" Jasmine was interrupted by scratching at the back door. Little Daisy was whining to come inside. Sam turned to let her in and spilled the remains of Jasmine's coffee on the counter. "I'll get this," Jasmine said. Sam went to let Daisy in while Jasmine wiped up the coffee. She reached to toss the spent paper towel in the trash and something shiny caught her eye. Jasmine glanced back to find Sam preoccupied toweling off an excited Daisy. She bent to get a better look at the shiny item in the trash. It looked like an EpiPen. Jasmine quickly flipped out her phone and snapped a couple of pictures. Her heart raced as she turned to find Sam with his back to her, hanging up the towel he'd been using moments ago. She let out a long breath.

"Sam, I'm going to get going. Call me if you need anything!" She called across the long galley kitchen. Sam waved and she thought she heard him say, "Thanks again," but she didn't stick around long enough to be sure.

Jasmine hopped in her Jeep and locked the doors. She yanked her phone from her coat pocket. She zoomed in on the photo she'd taken of Sam Day's garbage can. There among the coffee grounds, was a bright yellow. Jasmine's heart was still racing.

If Lily Day had been exposed to horsehair or dander after her performance Saturday night, that EpiPen could have saved her life. What was it doing in the trash? Further… hadn't Detective Williams said the investigating officers hadn't found an EpiPen in either the dressing room or the Day household?

Where had it been when they completed their search? Merritt Valley PD didn't investigate many homicides, but Jasmine didn't think they could miss a bright yellow auto-injector on the top of the garbage right there in the kitchen. Maybe the killer had hidden the EpiPen from Lily so they could intentionally cause her allergic reaction without the lifesaving medication. Maybe they had kept the pen hidden until after the police search. Jasmine's head was swimming with possible scenarios. She decided to bring this to Detective Williams straight away.

Jasmine parked in front of the Merritt Valley City Courthouse at 11:20 am. The stately old building also housed the city's police department and had a county sheriff's office. Jasmine couldn't remember the last time she'd been in this building, maybe to file paperwork last year. She was studying a list of office numbers on the wall when a familiar serious female voice surprised her.

"Lost, Dr. Cline?" Detective Williams was in a stylish and well cut suit this morning. Jasmine had hardly noticed the young detective's looks upon their other meetings. In the suit, however, Jasmine noticed she was tall and trim, she clearly spent a lot of time in a gym. She was pretty with classic features, smooth blonde hair which she wore shoulder-length and parted on the side. Williams was wearing makeup today, which complimented the pantsuit. Of course, she still had her utility belt on, but it was mostly concealed by her black blazer.

"I was looking for you," Jasmine replied.

"Ah. Looks like you found me. What can I do for you?" Williams almost smiled.

"Well I have something to show you, is there someplace we can talk?"

"Sure follow me." Williams led the way through a heavy oak door with no label. They seemed to be entering the police station from a back entrance. They passed a room with huge photos of the notes Sam Day had received from a mysterious admirer pinned to a whiteboard with notes all over it. They walked through a series of desks where officers seemed to be compiling lists and flipping through files. Jasmine was surprised to see such a large force in Merritt, though she'd never given the town's police force much thought.

They came to the room with Williams' name painted on the glass window. Detective Williams held the door open for Jasmine and closed it behind them.

"Now, what did you want to show me?" Williams asked and leaned back against her desk.

"Oh, yes." Jasmine pulled her phone from its pocket. "I saw this in the trash at Sam Day's this morning." Jasmine handed her phone over. Williams pinched the image to zoom.

"That's an EpiPen," Williams stated the obvious. She pressed a button on the phone on her desk. "Tucker get in here." Williams passed the cell phone back to Jasmine. Officer Tucker opened the door behind Jasmine.

"Oh hey, Jasmine." He smiled and turned his attention to Williams. "What's up?"

"I need you to take an officer and go check out the kitchen trash at the Day house, asap. Come to think of it, check all the trash cans, who knows what else was missed in the initial search." Williams looked annoyed but her tone was matter of fact as usual.

"You got it. Am I looking for something in particular?" Tucker asked.

"I think you'll know it when you see it," Williams responded.

"Okie Dokey." Tucker nodded to Jasmine and left.

"I'm going to need you to send me that photo," Williams said frankly.

"Sure." Jasmine took care of that immediately.

"I was going to call you after the press conference but since you're already here I'd like to get some prints from you before you leave." Williams checked the time as she said this.

"I'm sorry, you mean fingerprints? Why?" Jasmine was taken aback.

"Well, you've touched a vital piece of evidence. The note Sam Day received the night of his wife's death."

“Oh. Of course. So it’s just a matter of record, then?” Jasmine didn’t care for Williams’ accusatory tone, yet again.

“It is a matter of record, but you’ve also been colluding with the victim’s husband since her death. You had information about her allergy that was hardly common knowledge. Since you’re a vet you’ve got ample access to horses, and of course, you can access the theatre quite easily thanks to your mom.” Williams rattled off.

“I’m confused. Are you saying I’m a suspect?” Jasmine crossed her arms over her chest.

“I’m just stating the facts, Dr. Cline.” Williams stood and motioned toward the door. “I've got to get outside to talk with the press. Please see Vanessa at the front desk, she’ll get your prints processed.” Williams said dismissively and exited the room before Jasmine could respond.

Jasmine could not believe that Williams implied she could be involved in Lily’s death. She took several deep breaths to collect herself. She guessed that it was Williams’s job to suspect everyone. That should ease her mind, but it didn’t. She made her way to the front desk. A tired looking young woman asked, “Can I help you?” and Jasmine explained she was there to be fingerprinted.

The young woman led Jasmine to a sterile room where she filled in some forms. Jasmine had expected ink pads, but instead, the young woman slowly rolled each of Jasmine’s fingers over a screen on a machine that looked rather like a copier. A nearby computer screen showed each of the prints as they were completed.

When they’d wrapped up Jasmine went out the front door of the station, through the main hall of the courthouse, and found herself on the stone front stairs of the classic building. A throng of reporters and camera crews crushed in around the foot of the stairs. Detective Williams was standing at a podium flanked by the Mayor, a sheriff, and a few uniformed officers. Nancy Vale was asking Williams a question. Jasmine stayed put just out of sight.

“Detective Williams, do you have a primary suspect?” Vale was asking.

“I’m not going to discuss details of this case as the investigation is ongoing. What I can tell you is that we’re working around the clock to bring this case to a close so that Mrs. Day’s family can find closure, and to ensure the safety of our community. Thanks for coming, everyone.” Williams nodded seriously and the Mayor took her place at the podium.

Jasmine took the opportunity to sneak down the stairs and around the crowd. She could hear the Mayor commenting that Merritt Valley was a safe town and all the activities of The Festival of Leaves would go on as planned. Once in her Jeep, she sucked in a deep breath. She couldn’t let Williams's comments get to her. It wasn’t personal, the Detective was just doing her job. The truth would come out, one way or another. Jasmine’s phone started to ring and vibrate in her pocket.

“Hello?” Jasmine heard her voice shake.

“Jasmine? Are you okay? What’s wrong? Eric sounded worried. Jasmine was so pleased to hear his voice.

“Oh, Eric. I’m okay. It’s been quite a morning is all.” She answered.

“Oh, well, I just stopped by your shop and Ellie said you’re out for the day. I thought maybe you were sick.” Eric’s concern hadn’t faded.

“No, no, I’m fine. I didn’t have any appointments today.” Jasmine tried to sound more cheerful.

“Me either. I thought you might like to go out to the orchards. I know it’s a tourist thing but I just thought- “

“I’d love to.” Jasmine interrupted. She didn’t need convincing.

“Really? Great. I could pick you up?”

"Okay, I've got to let Francis out. My place? In an hour?" Jasmine wanted to collect herself a little.

"Perfect I'll see you soon." Eric hung up and Jasmine sighed audibly. She was relieved to know she'd see him soon. She started the Jeep to head home. Nancy Vale crossed in front of the Jeep. She recognized Jasmine and waved for her to stop. Jasmine rolled down the window.

"Hi, Dr. Cline. Do you have time tomorrow to do a little update on that dog?" Nancy asked brightly.

"Oh, sure. Maybe in the afternoon?" Jasmine had forgotten all about that.

"Sounds great. I think the town could use a fluff piece. How's he doing?" the journalist asked.

"Who?" Jasmine asked, confused.

"The dog, of course," Nancy replied.

"Oh of course. Yes. He's doing great. He's healing up quickly." and he likes to sleep on my pillow, Jasmine thought.

"I'm pleased to hear it. I'll let you get going, see you tomorrow!" Nancy waved and scurried off to her news van.

Jasmine was happy to get home. She started some water for tea and took Francis out. She let him sniff and wander around as much as he liked, she didn't like leaving him cooped up in the porch while she was away. For his part, Francis didn't seem to mind.

She poured him some fresh water and made herself a cup of chamomile tea. She sat over the cup at her kitchen table, still wearing her coat. Thoughts were swirling in her head. She knew a run would help her clear her head but there wasn't time, maybe this evening.

One thing was bothering her. That EpiPen. Sam was the one person who definitely knew about Lily's allergy before she was killed. So if he had thrown out that auto-injector or hidden it from Lily, he was almost definitely the killer. But if Sam killed Lily, why didn't he just allow the officials to rule her death an accident?

Jasmine inhaled the tea and sipped it slowly. Something didn't add up. And she was going to find out what it was. Jasmine enjoyed her tea and took some more deep breaths. When she finally relaxed, she heard a knock at the door. She turned to see Eric Canton's handsome face peering through her front door window. She grinned and called out; "Come in!"

Eric was dressed in his work boots, well-worn jeans, and a beige henley and canvas jacket. His blonde waves moved in the wind and his smile made Jasmine's troubles all melt away.

"Hi, sorry I'm early." Eric closed the door but lingered near it. Jasmine got up to greet him.

"You are?" Jasmine threw her arms around him for a hug and he gave her a good squeeze. She stayed there in his arms a minute, taking time to enjoy the embrace and get a good look at him. He grinned.

"I am. You ready?" He asked.

"Definitely." Jasmine led Francis back to the porch and he took up residence on his fleece bed. She grabbed her keys and she and Eric were off on another adventure, as Moira would put it.

The drive out to the orchards was beautiful. The skies were dappled with cloud cover, but soft streaks of Autumn sunlight fell across rolling hills, and fields strewn with brilliantly colored leaves. Eric slid a hand across the bench of his pickup truck and took Jasmine's hand.

"What did you do with your day off?" Eric asked.

"Oh, I just took a casserole over for Sam Day. He doesn't have much family here in town. Then I found some evidence that might implicate him for murder. And right before you called, I got fingerprinted at the police station. What about you?" Jasmine spat out.

"Wait, wait, wait. They fingerprinted you? Why?" Eric implored, incredulous.

"Well, I touched one of those mystery notes Sam got. And according to Detective Williams, I had the knowledge and access to have…" Jasmine trailed off.

"They can't possibly think you're a suspect." Eric was flabbergasted.

"No, I don't think she really does," Jasmine assured.

"That would just be ridiculous. What about the evidence you said you found?"

"There was an EpiPen in the trash at Sam's house," Jasmine answered.

"Oh wow. An EpiPen would have saved Lily that night. So if Sam threw it away…"

"That means he's the killer." Jasmine finished.

"Jazz, I don't think you should go over to his house anymore. At least not alone. He could be dangerous." There was concern in Eric's voice again.

“I think you’re right.” Jasmine agreed.

They pulled into a cornfield which served as a makeshift parking lot this time of year. Eric hopped out of the truck and as Jasmine opened her door to make that leap, he stepped up to the door and helped her down, hands around her waist. He set her down easily. For a moment Jasmine felt like the heroine in an old western.

Hand in hand they made their way to a large booth with prices scrawled across big blackboards. You could pick Honey Crisp or Cortland apples for six dollars a pound. A sweet-faced older woman in denim overalls handed them woven buckets and gave them a brief lesson on apple picking. She pointed out the paths to take and let them know there were quite a few honey crisp left.

Jasmine and Eric lost the afternoon picking apples and just walking the endless rows of apple trees. They talked about their families and work, and the craziest things animals had done while they were caring for them. They snuck a few small kisses in when no one was looking.

They had several pounds of apples by the time they made it back to the booth. They paid for them though Jasmine had no idea what they’d do with so many apples. The older woman helped them pack their apples in big burlap bags and Eric set the bags in the back of the truck. He opened Jasmine’s door for him and she surprised him by jumping up to the high seat herself. He laughed.

“What on earth are we going to do with all those apples?” Eric echoed Jasmine’s thoughts.

“Hm. Well, I could make an apple crisp tonight, if you’re game.” She suggested.

“Oh, I’m game.” Eric replied, “but what do we do with the other 45 pounds?” he exaggerated.

Jasmine laughed. "Well, Moira is a great cook, we should give her some. And maybe our mothers?"

Eric nodded. "That's a great idea. You have a grill, right?"

"I do, but I've never actually used it," she confessed and Eric chuckled.

"Let's change that today. I'll grill some steaks and veggies, and you make dessert?" He made the turn back toward Merritt.

"You've got a deal." Jasmine smiled. "The only problem is I'm supposed to be going for a run this afternoon."

Eric nodded toward the seat behind him, where there was a black gym bag. "I don't want to be presumptuous, but I could join you if you don't mind."

"Sounds great to me, if you can keep up." They both laughed. Jasmine loved these impromptu dates. Eric pulled into the parking lot at the grocery store.

"I'll just run in. Steaks, veggies, anything else?" Eric asked as he unbuckled his seat belt.

"Vanilla ice cream. For the apple crisp." Jasmine requested.

"Yum." Eric leaned over and gave her a tiny kiss before stepping out of the truck. Jasmine took the moment to check her phone. She had a message from her mom.

“Coffee? - mom.” was all the message said. Jasmine scrolled through the selfies she and Eric had snapped at the orchard. They were smiling and making silly faces in most of them. Jasmine paused at the photo she’d snapped of them kissing. She was just about to snap one of them laughing, she was up on a ladder and Eric was standing on the ground. They were close to the same height. Eric pretended to pose for the photo but when she snapped it he turned and kissed her. She just loved the picture. Not appropriate to send to mom though, so she chose a cute grinning picture and typed out a response.

“Sorry mom, something came up. Apple picking. Tomorrow?”

“Yay! Tomorrow is fine. Have fun! - mom.” She slipped her phone back into her pocket and looked around at the busy grocery parking lot. She saw a few people she recognized and lots of out-of-towners. Then she saw a familiar dark rain poncho get out of a pale blue hybrid. The hood wasn’t up and Jasmine recognized Vicki Andrews. She didn’t know why she hadn’t put that together the other morning.

Could it have been Vicki sending those notes to Sam Day? Jasmine wondered. She didn’t have much time to consider it because Eric suddenly opened his driver's side door. She turned to smile at him.

Back at Jasmine’s house, she and Eric got dinner ready as if they’d cooked together a thousand times. Eric started the grill and rubbed the steaks down with some salt. Jasmine got out a couple of cutting boards and set to work slicing apples. Eric cut the veggies right beside her and stuck them on skewers. Jasmine got the apple crisp ready and in the oven while Eric grilled in her backyard. Once she had popped the dish in the oven and set a timer, she grabbed her jacket to join him. She found him standing at the grill chatting with Francis like they were old friends. He had the big dog’s leash looped around his belt. Jasmine smiled.

Too chilly to eat outside, they enjoyed dinner at the small table in the kitchen. Their easy laughter filled Jasmine’s house. She couldn’t believe she’d been pouting at this very table only hours ago. She didn’t even scold Eric for sneaking Francis small chunks of steak.

They decided to wait until later for dessert. Jasmine set it on the counter to cool and joined Eric on her couch, where he was watching the local news. There was Detective Williams, telling Nancy Vale that they'd opened a homicide investigation in the mysterious death of Lily Day. The Mayor must have mentioned how safe a town Merritt Valley was half a dozen times when he had the floor. A Sheriff Jasmine didn't recognize also spoke. He said the sheriff's department had been alerted to a missing woman in nearby Gilbert but there was no reason to believe her disappearance was related to Mrs. Day's death. The Sheriff's Department would cooperate with MPD offering any assistance they could to resolve her case.

Jasmine seemed to remember Ellie telling her something about a missing woman in Gilbert. She scooted closer to Eric. They watched tv for a bit to digest before their run. Eric switched the channel and they settled on a pet rescue reality show. Eric draped an arm around Jasmine.

An hour passed and then two, the sun was setting.

"I guess we better hit that trail if we're going to run tonight," Eric said. Jasmine nodded in agreement. The trail was scattered with light posts, but the temperature would drop quickly as night fell.

"You can change in the guest room, it's at the end of the hall." She motioned down the short hall. "I'll be right out." Jasmine went to her room and changed into her running gear. When she emerged she found Eric in a fitted athletic shirt with long sleeves and loose-fitting joggers. His shirt revealed more defined muscle than Jasmine expected, he looked like a superhero. Jasmine realized she was starring, and worse, she realized Eric had noticed. She cleared her throat, and Eric chuckled.

"Shall we?" He gestured for her to go ahead. They left Francis behind in the enclosed porch. Together Jasmine and Eric stretched and warmed up, and they hit the trail at an easy pace. Jasmine thought it might be hard to run with Eric who was nearly a full foot taller than herself, but he matched her pace and they ran side by side. At first, they could chat easily but they sped up as they moved along the path, and soon they were just running together in comfortable silence. They paused at the lookout, though it was too dark to enjoy the view.

Jasmine noticed she was pushing herself harder than usual. It felt good. She glanced over at Eric who had broken a sweat. She was glad to see she wasn't the only one pushing harder. As they ran she let herself daydream a little. She imagined days and nights spent laughing together. Maybe morning runs, coffee shared over patient lists, and veterinary journals. Meals made together like tonight. Small adventures together, and quiet nights in.

Jasmine was just starting to wonder if Eric saw a similar future for them when she heard Francis barking frantically. She and Eric exchanged a glace and sped up. Eric got to the back door first and bounded inside with Jasmine close behind. Francis was barking at the door to the house, jumping and scraping at it fiercely. Eric wrangled the big dog and tried to settle him down. Jasmine brushed past them both and barged into her house. She got into the living room just in time to see the door to a small car shut. Whomever it had been sped off so quickly Jasmine was sure there would be marks left on the street. She turned to find Eric flipping on lights, making sure there was no one in the house. She grabbed her phone and dialed 911.

As Eric flicked on the large overhead light in the living room, Jasmine saw the small envelope on the floor. It had been dropped through her mail slot. "Eric!" she called and pointed at it. Someone answered on the other line.

"Hello, this is Jasmine Cline and 5656 Hattrick Avenue. I've just had well… not a break in exactly. But I received a note similar to the ones Sam Day received before his wife was killed." Jasmine explained to dispatch.

When she hung up Jasmine bent and picked up the small envelope. It wasn't sealed. She slid the card out and took a deep breath.

"Keep away from my Sam.
You don't know who I am.
Do you value your life?
Might end up like his wife."

Jasmine gasped. Eric took the note from her and read it himself.

"I think I'd better stay here tonight." Eric's tone was serious. Jasmine nodded.

Within minutes Officer Tucker was sitting with Jasmine at her kitchen table. Eric made some coffee and generally hovered about.

“So you didn’t get a look at his face?” the officer was asking.

“No, I didn’t see anyone, just the car,” Jasmine answered.

“Pity.” Officer Tucker took some notes. Another officer entered through the back door. “No sign of anyone sir. No sign of a break-in, either.” Officer Tucker nodded.

“I said they didn’t break-in, just left the note,” Jasmine interjected.

“I know. No need to panic, I’m sure it's nothing to worry about.” the officer responded.

“All due respect, officer, but the last woman to get a note like that is dead,” Eric interjected, irritated. Jasmine had never heard that menacing timber in his voice before.

“You’re right.” Detective Williams called from the front door. “I’m sorry Dr. Cline, but we won’t let anything happen to you. Can I see the note?” Williams joined them at the table. Tucker passed her the note and got up to get some coffee. Williams read the note over a few times.

“Hm.” was all she said.

“Hm?” Jasmine echoed. Officer Tucker came back and passed both of the women coffee cups.

“I was just thinking that unless Sam Day has a personality disorder or a secret male lover, we’re probably looking for a woman.” Williams slid the note into an evidence bag with her gloved hand. She tugged the blue latex gloves off and picked up her coffee.

"If you're about to suggest I wrote these notes me-" Jasmine began.

"I'm not suggesting that at all, Dr. Cline," Williams assured. "The Sheriff and I spent all day going over the profiles of the cast and crew. Two women have made inappropriate suggestive comments to or about Sam, according to witnesses. Molly Stephens joked that she could easily steal Sam from Lily, on more than one occasion. Several people insist she was only joking and she has a sparkling clean record. The other woman is-"

"Vicki Andrews." Jasmine finished. Williams's eyes narrowed.

"Yes, Vicki Andrews. She's made some comments about Sam's good looks and made some unkind comments about Lily's looks during dress rehearsals. So far there's no material evidence on either." Williams took a long sip of her coffee.

"So one of the women was jealous of Lily Day or interested in her husband. It's all quite tragic, but what does it have to do with Jasmine?" Eric asked, resting hands on each of Jasmine's shoulders. Williams noticed the gesture and took Eric in.

"Eric… Canton, right?" Eric nodded. "Well, my guess is that Jasmine has gotten too close to this case for comfort. Twice now, she has presented evidence that brings us closer to finding them out. And of course, she's seen Sam twice in as many days." Williams set her cup down firmly.

"What about Sam? What do you think about the EpiPen?" Jasmine queried.

"I'm not sure yet, Jasmine. I hope you don't mind if I call you that." Williams was sincere.

"I think we may as well be on a first-name basis." Jasmine smiled weakly.

Williams offered a hand. "Cassie." She shook Jasmine's hand and stood up. "We're going to set up a watch for you tonight, there will be a squad outside. Call me if you remember anything." Williams took her leave and Officer Tucker was close behind.

"Sorry, Jasmine. We're going to find them, I promise." Tucker offered as he left. Eric took his seat at the table and took Jasmine's hand.

"I hope you don't mind if I stay here tonight," Eric repeated.

"I don't mind." Jasmine swirled her coffee in her cup.

"I'll take the couch." Eric offered.

"You'll have to. Francis takes up most of my bed." She smiled. Francis perked at his name and came over to rest his chin in her lap. She stroked his head and whispered sweet things to him about what a good boy he was. Eric collected empty coffee cups and washed them. When he finished up he turned to Jasmine.

"I don't know about you but I could use a shower. You mind?"

"Of course not. There are towels and things in the cabinet in the bathroom. I'm afraid I don't think any of my things will fit you." Jasmine got up and checked the locks on the doors. She wasn't easily shaken but having a murderer threaten her life was unnerving. Eric bent to kiss her forehead.

"I've got some things in my bag. I won't be long." He assured. Jasmine guessed he had to be prepared with changes of clothes for his work, just as she did. Working with animals on farms was messy work.

She sat back down at the kitchen table and sipped her coffee. What a night. A threat from an unknown killer was unsettling. She was deeply relieved Eric was there with her. It was also a relief that the professionals seemed to be zeroing in on some suspects. Jasmine set her cup down and rubbed her temples. All that could wait until tomorrow. She decided to take a shower herself and hoped the hot water tank in her small house could handle both showers running.

Jasmine wrapped her hair, it didn't need to be washed today. She took a quick hot shower. The hot water tank seemed up to the task, and the steamy water relaxed her tense muscles. After she'd had enough, she toweled off and put on a soft lavender nightdress and matching full-length robe. She sprayed a little warm vanilla scented perfume on her pulse points and gently unbraided her hair. Her hair was full of waves, spilling over the lavender. She loved creams and pastels, they paired nicely with her warm olive skin. She gave herself a once over and though she did look rather worn out, she was satisfied with her reflection.

Jasmine found Eric already on the couch. His hair curled slightly when it was wet. She had expected him to be watching tv but found him studying something on his phone. She sank into the couch beside him and he glanced over.

"Wow. Do you always look this beautiful before bed?" Eric stammered.

"I try." Jasmine teased and gave him a quick kiss. "What are you up to?"

"I was reading about the suspects," Eric answered. "I found something interesting."

"Oh? What did you find?"

Eric leaned closer so Jasmine could see the screen as well. "Vicki Andrews was in two other plays with Sam and Lily. In Minneapolis. Both were supporting roles, and Lily had a leading role. Look." He flipped through some cast photos.

“Well, that could explain how she got so… obsessed with Sam.” Jasmine thought out loud.

“That’s what I was thinking.” Eric agreed. “She’s even staring at him in some of these photos.” He pinched one photo to zoom and though the photo was low quality, Vicki seemed to be gaping at Sam Day, who was performing in the center of the stage.

“When was this taken?” Jasmine asked. Eric took a moment to find the date.

“Almost two years ago.”

“That’s a long time. Maybe she resented Lily for years.” Jasmine considered.

“Maybe.” Eric set his phone aside and turned to face her. “How are you holding up? You’ve had quite a day.” There was that concerned tone again.

“Oh, I’m alright. I am grateful that you’re here. And at least that note means I’m not on the suspect list anymore.” Jasmine tugged at one of her sleeves. Eric touched her cheek. She looked up into his dark blue eyes.

“It’s going to be okay, Jazz. I promise.” Something about the way Eric said that she believed him. They watched some silly reality show for a while and Eric stretched out. She relaxed in his arms, a cheek pressed against his chest. His familiar scent of cedar and soap was comforting. Before she knew it, Jasmine was sound asleep.

Suddenly Jasmine found herself out running the trail behind her house. It was raining but she didn't feel wet. She was running but she couldn't tell where she was on the trail. Jasmine felt disoriented and frightened. She turned to look behind her and get her bearings. There was a figure in a dark blue rain poncho running towards her, impossibly fast. Though it should be easy to see, she couldn't make out their face. Jasmine turned to run from the figure and she couldn't pick up enough speed. She glanced over her shoulder and the figure was gaining on her. Jasmine tripped on something on the trail. She fell but didn't hit the ground. She felt herself falling and falling, endlessly. She looked down and saw the valley below, suddenly the ground seemed to be rushing toward her. She was going to slam into the rocky forest floor.

Jasmine woke with a start. It was pitch black she couldn't see a thing. She gasped, she felt like she was still flying, she couldn't feel anything beneath her.

"Shhh shhh, you're okay," Eric whispered in the dark. She realized Eric was carrying her. "You had a nightmare." He set her down on the bed and turned on the lamp on her nightstand.

"Oh god. I felt like I was falling and I woke up still flying!" Jasmine explained.

"Sorry about that. We fell asleep. Your dream woke me up, I thought you might be more comfortable in bed." Eric fussed with blankets and pillows.

"Thank you. What time is it?" Jasmine still felt a little disoriented.

"Nearly six am," Eric answered.

"Oh, it's just about time to start the day. Lay with me a minute?" Eric crawled onto the bed and gathered her up. They lay together for a few minutes, just resting. Jasmine felt Francis leap onto the bed. She and Eric chuckled together.

The morning went just as Jasmine had daydreamed while running with Eric the day before. She made coffee, Eric made toast. They got ready and enjoyed their breakfast together with ease. The only thing wrong with this picture was the police car she noticed out the front window. She fed Francis and while she was getting her coat on, Eric clipped his leash in place. She turned to find Eric giving Francis a prep talk about his day.

"You're going to be on the news today. Just act natural, everyone will love you. If the news lady makes you nervous, don't picture her naked, that will just make it worse. Just smile big for the cameras. Okay, buddy?" Eric scratched Francis's head.

Jasmine laughed and Eric grinned. "You ready?" She asked him. He nodded. They paused on the sidewalk where their vehicles were parked. An officer nodded from his car window across the street.

"Text me?" Eric asked. "And call if… if anything comes up." If any murderers leave me ominous poetry, Jasmine thought.

"I will. Have a good day today." She tiptoed up to reach him and gave him a long slow kiss. She felt his lips smile.

As Jasmine sat in her Jeep with Francis and watched Eric drive off with a wave, she wondered what the day would bring. All she knew right then was that, if she had to face a challenging day, a morning with Eric had been the best way to start it.

CHAPTER NINE

When Jasmine got to work Tuesday morning, there was a news van parked out front of the office. She was perplexed by this since she was meant to be interviewed by Nancy Vale in the afternoon. She shrugged and pulled around back, her police escort followed. She waved to the officer as she got out of her Jeep and took Francis inside. She dropped off her things in her office and made her way to the front desk.

"Morning Boss!" Ellie exclaimed from behind the desk. The lobby was full of people but rather than patients, it was a full camera crew, sound people, and of course, Nancy.

"I'm sorry we're so early, Dr. Cline. We have another story to cover this afternoon so I thought we'd come to see you bright and early!" Nancy was almost as cheery as Ellie in the morning.

"It's okay. At least my hair and makeup are fresh." Jasmine smiled.

"Great! This spot isn't live so, relax. We can always film again and edit things together if we need to." Nancy assured.

They decided to set up in front of the business, with the signage behind Jasmine, Nancy, and Francis. A little free advertising. They set up some straw bales for Nancy and Jasmine to sit on. The crew fussed with lights and roped off the sidewalk around them. A few people were gathering to see what the commotion was about. Someone adjusted Jasmine's coat and scarf, then clipped a small mic on her collar before tucking in a battery pack in the folds of her jacket. A man with a camera counted down with his fingers and then pointed at Nancy Vale.

“Good afternoon from Merritt Valley Mobile Animal Clinic. I’m here with Dr. Jasmine Cline, a local vet, who you may remember helped rescue our furry friend here this weekend. Dr. Cline, how is the dog doing after his ordeal?” Nancy turned her attention to Jasmine.

“Just Jasmine, please. He’s doing great.” Jasmine crouched down near Francis and the cameraman pushed on them. “His injuries were minor and he’s healing well. As you can see he’s already gaining some weight. And he’s well trained, he even knows a few tricks.”

“That’s wonderful news, Dr. Cline. I wonder if you might show us a few of those tricks?” Nancy requested, right on cue.

Jasmine nodded and produced some treats from her pocket and since Francis was already sitting, she said, “Shake!” Francis hammed it up, he shook and even high-fived her hand. Nancy and the watching crowd clapped. Jasmine slipped him a treat and said, “Lay down!” Again, Francis complied.

On a whim, Jasmine called, “Rollover!” At which Francis rolled over, hopped up and gave a pleasant, “woof!” The crowd celebrated while Francis enjoyed his treats. His tail wagged happily, he ate up the attention as well as the tasty treats.

“There you have it, folks, this just goes to show you a rescued dog is a happy dog.” Nancy emphasized “rescued” and Jasmine was pleased she had.

“Dr. Cline, has anyone come forward to claim their missing dog?” Nancy inquired.

“Unfortunately, no one has. We’ve contacted all the local shelters to get the word out that we’ve found him. Rather than leave him with a shelter, I’ve opted to care for him myself until his owner can be found.” Jasmine explained, trying to speak slowly despite her nerves.

“What will happen to him if no one comes forward to claim him?” Vale questioned.

“Well, I suppose we will work with a shelter to find him a lovely forever home,” Jasmine responded. Francis stepped up onto her hay bale and slurped her face. Jasmine giggled.

“Looks like he may have found a willing home already,” Nancy interjected.

“Yes, maybe he has.” Jasmine agreed.

“When you’re not rescuing stranded dogs, what is it you do here at Merritt Valley Mobile Animal Clinic?” Nancy didn’t miss a beat.

“Uhm. Well, we treat domestic pets of all kinds. Dogs, cats, birds, reptiles, even guinea pigs. As the name implies, we’re a mobile clinic too, so we’re happy to come treat your pet right in the comfort of your home.” Jasmine tried not to sound too much like a commercial.

“That must be a great convenience to your customers.” Nancy encouraged.

“Yes, it’s especially nice for seniors and people with mobility issues. Or people who have senior pets, of course.”

“It sounds just wonderful. I’d like to thank you on behalf of all of us at KBRT, Dr. Cline. Thank you for taking the time to chat with us here today.” Nancy finished and the camera seemed to focus on her. Jasmine sighed with relief.

“We’re reporting from Merritt Valley Mobile Animal Clinic here on Grand Avenue. This report was brought you by the Festival of Leaves giving committee. While you’re out enjoying the Festival, stop in, say hello to Dr. Cline, and book an appointment for your four-legged friends. I’m Nancy Vale with KBRT News.” Nancy finished and sat still for several moments before the cameraman signaled to her. She relaxed and turned to Jasmine.

“That was great!” she exclaimed. “I don’t think we need to reshoot, do you?” Before Jasmine could answer she continued; “That was just perfect, Jasmine, you’re a natural. And those dog tricks! This was exactly the piece we needed.” Nancy finally seemed to come up for air.

"Oh good. I don't know about being a natural, but I'm glad we're finished." Jasmine said flatly. "Francis does put on a good show, though, huh?"

"He really does." Nancy patted Francis but kept her distance. Jasmine figured the journalist couldn't afford to muss her clothes since she'd have to be on camera all day. Nancy rose and swiped loose bits of straw from her clothes. "Thanks again, Jasmine. I'll send you the piece after it airs tonight, you might want to share it around on your social media."

"Oh that's perfect, thank you." Jasmine hadn't even thought of that but it would be great press for the clinic. She stood and tapped straw off her own clothes. While she was straightening herself out, she overheard someone from Nancy's staff whispering in a panic. She could only pick up a few words here and there.

"Sounds like they're making an arrest.... We've got to get over to... yeah we'll break the story, let's go." This short fellow in a headset was in an awful hurry. Whatever he was saying prompted the rest of the crew to hustle up all their equipment. Someone nearly snatched the mic off of Jasmine's coat. In mere minutes the whole crew was gone in a flurry of cameras and lights. The news van fired up and whooshed into the busy street.

Jasmine rushed to the Jeep and hopped in as Francis leaped up and over her into the passenger seat. She thought briefly that they were becoming quite the team before she shooed him into the back and turned the ignition.

Jasmine pulled into the street. She let a few cars turn to provide cover between herself and the news van. She wanted to see where they were off to, and she didn't want them to notice her. She was careful to leave some distance between them as they made their way through town, and it wasn't until she saw blue and red light reflecting off the houses and trees, that she realized they were in the neighborhood where the Days lived. She slowed down to a crawl and watched as the van pulled up behind several squads and an unmarked police vehicle, all of which had their lights going.

Jasmine was grateful they had left their sirens off. She pulled over and parked a block behind the van and law enforcement vehicles. She pulled out her phone, hoping to use the zoom on her phone to get a better view of the action. She watched as Nancy Vale and her cameraman hopped out of the van and hurried across the street to the Day's front steps before being promptly stopped by two uniformed officers. Even from a block away, Jasmine could see Nancy crank up her megawatt smile and try to charm the officers into allowing her closer to the scene.

Francis distracted Jasmine from the hottest news story in Merritt Valley with a low growl. She followed his gaze out the passenger side window and noticed a grey hooded figure was also watching the show. Without thinking, she lifted her phone and snapped a photo. Jasmine glanced over to the house, where Nancy was beginning to film and realized that the mystery hoodie couldn't be seen from where the anchorwoman and police officers were standing. When she turned her attention back to the unknown person, they were staring straight at her. Jasmine's breath caught in her throat. Though their face was in shadow and covered by a pair of huge sunglasses, their mouth was set in a firm, menacing scowl. Jasmine felt herself sweating. She swiveled in her seat and snuck a quick peek behind herself, maybe they were looking at something else.

As she flipped back to the mystery hoodie, they gestured to their eyes and then pointed at her as if to say, "I'm watching you."

A cold chill ran down Jasmine's back. She kept her eyes on the stranger as she fumbled for the shifter and just as she was about to hit the gas and drive off, they looked back at the Days' house. Jasmine caught sight of Detective Williams and some other officers exiting the house with Sam Day. He didn't seem to be wearing handcuffs and merely walked between the officers. Williams appeared to say some very brief remarks to Nancy Vale before the entire party started to enter police vehicles and drive off.

Jasmine glanced back at the house where the mystery hoodie was hiding, but they were gone without a trace.

CHAPTER TEN

Jasmine parked out front of the clinic and clicked for Francis who followed her out into the street. Another squad car was parked in the alley. Though it was empty, the engine was still running.

Jasmine wondered why a police officer would be parked right beside the animal clinic before she remembered that Detective Williams had promised her that they'd be looking in on her since she'd received open threats. Ooops.

She scrambled inside to find a young female officer, Jasmine's mother Donna, and Claire all standing around Ellie who seemed to be on a mission with her cell phone. The room gave out a collective sigh as she walked in.

"Where did you GO?" Donna rushed to hug her as if she'd just survived a battle. Everyone else crushed in close, too.

"I just had an errand to run," Jasmine thought it best to leave out her amateur sleuth mission for now. "What on earth has you all so worried?"

"I'm sorry, that's my fault." the young officer spoke up. "I lost track of you when the news team took off, and then I asked Ellie where you were."

"And then I stopped by to see if you wanted lunch and no one could find you!" Donna sighed, exasperated. Francis leapt up, trying to lick her face.

Jasmine shooed the dog down and gestured for her mom to sit on the lobby sofa. She sighed softly herself. "I'm sorry, I completely forgot that the police would be checking on me. I'm okay, I promise. I'm sorry I worried you all." She smiled, trying to reassure the women.

Claire was convinced, she nodded and wandered back toward her office. Ellie went back to her phone, and the officer stepped toward the front door.

“I’ll just be outside if you need me.” she ducked out.

“Whew,” Jasmine sighed again, relieved. “What’s going on there, Ellie?” She peered over the big desk.

“Well, they just arrested Sam Day.” Ellie was watching a local Livestream. She lifted the screen so Jasmine could see. It was hard to make anything out, the video was disjointed and bouncing around.

“Oh about that. I have a phone call to make. Mom, can I meet you for lunch in a bit?” Jasmine smiled. “I’ve got some calls to make and then I’ll be over. Maybe 20 minutes?”

Donna nodded. “I’m going to take my grand puppy with me.” She scooped up Francis’ leash and they headed out together.

Back in her office, Jasmine dialed Detective Williams. She assumed she would go to voicemail since the Detective was busy, and she was right.

“Hi, this is Jasmine Cline. I saw something this afternoon that you should know about, give me a call when you have time.” She ended the call, sat on the edge of her desk, and flipped open her texts. A pile from her mom, one from Claire, 2 from Ellie. All of them said something similar to, “WHERE ARE YOU!?”

She skipped to 3 unread texts from Eric.

“Hey Beautiful, you’ll do great on tv today. Break a leg.”

“I mean, don’t actually break a leg.”

“But if you do I have plaster. Xoxo”

Jasmine giggled. Murder, tv interviews, and threats from an ominous hooded stalker, and she was still able to giggle. What sort of magic was that man made of? She couldn't think of a cute response so she snapped a selfie and sent it with the message.

"Thanks for the smile, needed that today!"

Jasmine checked the time. 12:30. No wonder she was hungry. She opened her photos and found the image she'd snapped of the hooded person watching Sam Day get escorted away by the cops.

The photo was taken at 11:43 am. Less than an hour ago. Even with zoom, Jasmine still couldn't make out much of their face with the hood and sunglasses. Even so, the mouth didn't look like Vicki Andrews. She wondered if Detective Williams had people who could clean the image up. She also wondered… how well could they make out her face inside her Jeep? Maybe they knew who that Jeep belonged to. Certainly, this was the same character leaving letters around town, scaring people. But, why? Jasmine could only come up with one answer.

They murdered Lily Day.

Suddenly Jasmine jumped up from her desk. She felt that same cold chill run down her spine. It struck her that getting the photo to Detective Williams probably shouldn't wait. She quickly gathered her things and dashed out to the parking lot.

Jasmine pulled up to the Merritt Valley City Hall at about 1 pm. As she strode through the front door she found Nancy Vale and several other local news people crowding around. Jasmine bumped and shoved her way through them and they hardly seemed to notice. They were crowding around the windows, trying to catch a glimpse of Merritt's top murder suspect.

Jasmine tapped on the window and an officer motioned to the door in the hall where he let her inside.

"Whew. It's like paparazzi out there," she laughed as he shut the door.

"You aren't kidding. It's been like that all afternoon." The officer smiled. "Are you here to see Detective Williams? She's pretty busy with the investigation."

"I am. I know she's busy but this can't wait." Jasmine responded.

"Okay, I'll let her know." He made his way through some cubicle to a back hall and Jasmine sat down. She hoped Detective Williams wouldn't be too annoyed at being interrupted. She'd like to stay on the detective's good side.

A few minutes passed before Detective Williams appeared with the officer who'd let Jasmine in.

"Jasmine." Cassandra Williams smiled and Jasmine released a sigh of relief. "While it's nice to see you, I'm sure you can see that we're quite busy here today."

"Oh I know you are and I'm sorry to interrupt, but this can't wait," Jasmine answered and glanced around to see that they were alone in the waiting area. She passed over her phone.

"I took this photo earlier today. I… I happened to be near the Day house when you picked up Sam earlier. Whoever this is was watching from across the street." Jasmine stammered nervously.

"You just happened to be in the area, huh?" Detective Williams gave Jasmine a look. She scrutinized the photo on the screen. "Hm. Can't make out who this is. Can you send me this photo?" She passed the phone back to Jasmine.

"Sure. After I snapped that they noticed me and made a sort of threatening gesture at me."

"Threatening?" Williams inquired.

"Yes like…" Jasmine trailed off and made the, I'm watching you motion, herself.

"Oh, that." Williams cleared her throat. "Jasmine I must advise you to stop poking around this case. We've got it under control and it's clear that it isn't safe for you." she said flatly.

"I… I will try not to." Jasmine said, honestly.

"Very well. Please send me that photo, we'll see what we can do. I think it's best if you don't stay alone tonight."

"You're probably right. I'll find someone to stay with me." Jasmine answered.

"Good. I've got to get back. Call or text if you, 'just happen,' upon anything else." Williams smirked and turned back down the short hall to what Jasmine assumed were interrogation-type rooms. She wondered if they had one-way mirrors, or if Sam Day was cuffed to a table back there, chain-smoking as officers barraged him with questions.

Jasmine shook her head at herself and made her way back through the throng of news people. A couple of them tried to get answers from her.

"How do you know Sam Day?" one asked.

"What ties do you have to the murder of Lily Day?" called another.

Jasmine squirmed and continued to fight her way through them. Nancy Vale suddenly appeared among them and a few moved out of her way.

"Hey, Jazz. Sorry for the hassle. Here let me help you." Nancy and her camera guy guided Jasmine through the growing crowd. The news must be spreading fast, every local newspaper and small tv or radio station seemed to be in the courthouse. The cameraman was an effective shield from prying reporters. They arrived at the doors.

"Thanks so much!" Jasmine called to them both as she made her way outside. "I owe you one!"

"I'll hold you to that!" Nancy cried after her. Jasmine believed she would.

Jasmine dug through her bag, looking for her keys. She very rarely misplaced anything and prided herself on being organized. She guessed all the commotion and stress of the last couple of days must be catching up to her. Finally, she grasped her keys. Out of the corner of her eye, she caught a grey hooded figure moving in a car near her Jeep. It was hard to ascertain at this distance but they looked an awful lot like the person who'd been watching her, and the police this morning.

Jasmine glanced at their license plate and then ducked into the doorway out of sight. She had no intention of wading back into that crowd but she didn't want mystery hoodie to see her again, either. She tapped out a text to Detective Williams. "Mystery Hoodie is out front. License plate 261-ABJ." Send. She hoped they could figure out who this person was, as soon as possible.

Jasmine peeked out from the doorway and as she hoped, Mystery Hoodie had driven away. Still, she made short work of getting across the lot to her vehicle. She hurried out of the lot and took the highway to avoid her usual routes around town. She stopped at the diner at the edge of town.

Jasmine couldn't remember when she'd eaten at that diner last. She didn't plan to eat there today, either, unfortunately. She just needed a place to collect her thoughts.

This morning had been pretty sure that Vicki Andrews had stalked Sam and Lily for a couple of years before ultimately killing Lily, maybe to make way for a romance with Sam. Jasmine had also guessed that it was Vicki Andrews she'd seen on the trail and at the grocery store the other day.

But if that was Vicki, who was this mystery person in the grey hoodie, watching in the wings and making threatening gestures? Something didn't add up. Jasmine recalled that Detective Williams had mentioned another woman with a suspicious interest in Sam Day. Molly something or other. Maybe it was time to check her out.

Jasmine sent her mom a text. "There was a Molly in the play, do you happen to know her last name?" Jasmine set the phone down on her center console. If Vicki hadn't killed Lily, the field was wide open for guesses as to who had. Jasmine wanted to narrow that field. She rested her head on the steering wheel a moment to think, hoping for a new angle.

A thought hit her abruptly. It wasn't a new angle she needed, she just needed to look deeper at the first one. She was going to have to pester her friend Moira at Blackbird once again. Jasmine turned her Jeep back on and pulled away from the diner. She caught a longing look at it before the old fashioned burger place faded out of sight. She needed to get a big greasy burger and fries there, soon.

Just as Jasmine pulled into her parking spot behind the animal clinic, her phone chimed, notifying her of a text received. It chimed again before she could put the Jeep in park and shut it off.

One text from her mom read; "Stephens, how come? Are you okay?- Mom."

Another, from Detective Williams; "Will look into it, thanks."

"Stephens, Stephens, Stephens," Jasmine recited to herself. Since the lot was empty aside from staff vehicles, she went straight down the alley and around the block to Blackbird. She entered the shop and was surprised to see a smartly dressed young man behind the counter instead of Moira. Silly, of course, Moira would have staff, she couldn't run that shop every day alone.

"Hello, anything I can help you find?" He called over the counter. Several other women and a couple of men were browsing but it was clear he was speaking to Jasmine.

"No, no, unless you know where to find Moira?" Jasmine assumed Moira had the day off.

"Oh yeah, she's in her office, you want me to run and get her?" He asked in a friendly, professional tone.

"Well if it's alright with you I'll just go back myself. I know the way and we're old friends." Jasmine answered.

"Oh sure that's okay." He went back to whatever he was up to. Jasmine shuffled down the hallway and tapped on the grand ornate door. Its bright teal color reminded her of the ruffled petticoats she'd seen Lily wearing the day they had bumped into each other at this boutique.

"Come on in," Moira announced from within. Jasmine opened the door and shut it at her back.

"Hi Moira, I'm sorry to interrupt." Jasmine offered.

"Silly, you're hardly interrupting. It's always nice to see you." Moira replied with a shining smile. "What can I do for you?"

"To be honest, I have another question about Lily Day." Jasmine found she was embarrassed suddenly. She sat down in front of her old friend's desk.

"If I didn't know better I'd say you're getting obsessed with this case, babe." Moira was always so direct.

"You know. I might agree with you." Jasmine confessed. "But, now I've got good reason. Last night someone slipped a threatening note under my door."

"A threatening note?" Moira was surprised.

"Yeah. Let me…" Jasmine trailed off and pulled out her phone. She'd snapped a photo of the notecard before the good Detective had taken it as evidence. She opened the photo and passed her phone to Moira. Moira took her time, appearing to read it over a couple of times.

"Jazz honey, this is downright disturbing. Please tell me you called the police." Moira was concerned.

"I did. It matches the notes Sam received before Lily…" Jasmine began.

"Before whoever wrote these notes killed her." Moira finished for her.

"Yes, probably. Listen, the reason I came is that her killer probably used a horsehair brush. I don't think they're very common anymore. I wondered if you have records of sales like that?" Jasmine wondered aloud. Moira contemplated this a moment.

"Well, if they just bought one off the sales floor, no. I do sometimes sell sets of makeup brushes and there's no way to track who bought which." Moira flipped through some notebooks and ledgers in her desk. "But," she continued, "If they made a special order in the last two years, it's in this book. She passed over a sizeable black record book.

"Rupert insists I should just utilize our point of sale software to keep these records, but I'm still a little old fashioned.

"I don't think anyone would ever call you old fashioned," Jasmine quipped. "You mind if I borrow this?"

"Not at all. But Jazz I don't think it's a good idea for you to stay alone tonight. If you're receiving threats," Moira started.

"That's not even all of it." Jasmine cut her off and Moira frowned. "I also saw a… suspicious character earlier while they were taking Sam into custody."

"Oh Jazz," Moira sighed. "You do know you're not a secret agent, right?" She continued before Jasmine could respond. "Just, come stay with me for a couple of days, please? There's plenty of space and I just don't think it's a good idea for you to stay alone with a killer eyeing you."

"You're right, of course. I wasn't alone last night, though." Jasmine started, there was a knock at the door and Rupert popped his head in.

"Sorry to interrupt you ladies, but Moira there's a woman who asked for you specifically. She's buying a big pile of dresses and wants your opinion on the accessories."

"I'll be right there." Moira waved and Rupert vanished. "So you'll come stay with me." She wasn't asking.

"Well, that's very kind of you, but what about Francis?" Jasmine suddenly remembered she had a dog.

"What about him? Bring him too." Moira wasn't going to take no for an answer. She slid a key off her keychain and passed it to Jasmine. "Now, that's settled. You can tell me all about your sleepover tonight. I'll be there by 5 but you feel free to stop in whenever you can." Moira slipped out of the room with a wave.

Jasmine rolled the key in her hand and clipped it onto her keyring. There was no arguing with Moira when she set her mind to something. Besides, she was right. The threats she had received were reason enough not to stay alone overnight. Jasmine had hoped to spend more time with Eric but that might start to feel like rushing a relationship. She sighed. She'd stay with Moira.

She snuck out of the shop and back into her office without bumping into any murderers in raincoats. Jasmine was beginning to resent this unknown person. She guessed the only way to get out from under this mess was to find out who they were, as soon as possible.

Francis glanced up at her from his spot on the floor and promptly resumed his nap. She closed her office door and sat down with the black record book. She started in 2016 and started to scan the pages for familiar names, brushes, or vanity sets. Jasmine buzzed through the pages quickly. This work was easy to her, reminiscent of her years studying medical terms and anatomy before she got into the veterinary program.

Jasmine made it through 2016 in just over an hour. No mention of Vicki Andrews or any interesting brushes. She wondered if perhaps this was a foolish errand. Though if she was honest with herself, having something tangible to focus on was easing her nerves.

Francis perked up when she sat back in her chair.

"You wanna go out?" She asked him. He stood up and wagged his tail which she took to mean yes. She gathered up her stuff and his leash. "C'mon, you." She said idly to Francis and shut off the lights.

After a short walk, she and Francis took the back alleys home. Jasmine realized with relief she'd lost her police escort. Though she took threats seriously, she felt she could look after herself. Besides, she had her trusty watchdog with her. She put the Jeep in park and stretched out an arm to stroke Francis. She was in danger, alright. In danger of falling in love twice this week.

Once inside Jasmine packed a backpack for Francis, first. His dishes, some kibble, and treats. She realized she hadn't gotten him any toys and made a mental note to do that this weekend. She wandered to her room and packed an overnight bag. The circumstances were less than desirable, but she had to admit she was excited to have a sleepover with an old friend. She had stayed overnight at the Randall's countless nights in high school.

Just as she zipped up her bag, her phone buzzed to alert her she had a new message. It was Moira.

"No time to cook tonight. Pizza?"

"Perfect." Jasmine wrote back. A girls' night with pizza and PJs sounded pretty amazing. She ticked off a mental list to make sure she had everything she needed and scooped up her bag. Francis was waiting for her, sitting next to his backpack. It was so cute Jasmine snapped a picture.

Jasmine checked the back door to ensure it was locked. She flipped the deadlock, scooped up Francis' leash and backpack and they were off. The sun was just setting as she locked the front door. An icy wind brushed her legs and tossed leaves wildly across her stone walkway. She'd have to switch out the leather jacket for something warmer, very soon.

Once she and Francis were settled in the Jeep, she turned it on but left it in park. She sat back and watched the sun set over Hattrick Avenue. Deep purples and hot pinks played across the horizon and illuminated the crimson and cayenne leaves of the oaks and maple trees that lined her quiet street. For a moment the leaves were so brilliant they seemed alight with fire. As swiftly as they began to blaze, the light and colors faded to pastels, and the sun set, leaving a heavenly violet in its wake. Jasmine sighed softly and glanced at Francis who seemed to be watching with her. They watched until the first stars appeared.

"Pretty great, huh? Sunsets are my favorite. This weekend we'll watch the sunrise, too." she promised.

CHAPTER ELEVEN

Jasmine had great timing. Though it was after 6 pm, she pulled up to Moira Randall's house just as Moira was shutting off her car.

"Oh, you've got good timing!" Moira called from the walk. Jasmine and Francis caught up, bags in tow.

"I thought I might be late," Jasmine confessed.

"Nonsense. I knew I'd be home later than usual tonight. It's so crazy at the store during the festival." Moira unlocked the front door and flicked on the lights. She disappeared down the hall, trailing off her heels as she went. "You remember the guest room, right? Make yourself at home I'm going to get changed. Pizza should be here any minute!" Her footsteps fell away.

Jasmine did remember the room she'd stayed in all those years ago. It was upstairs, the second room on the right. She climbed the beautifully crafted grand staircase. While the house was very familiar, all the art and lighting had been updated. There were bright modern paintings and abstract sculptures everywhere she looked. Jasmine passed what had been Moira's parents' room, so many years ago. Now it seemed to be a sewing studio. She hadn't even considered that Moira sewed or designed clothes, herself.

She found the guest bedroom had an update, too. A huge painting of vivid flowers hung over the bed, which was dressed mostly in white. The throw pillows were in the same vivid colors as the painting. She unpacked so her things wouldn't be too wrinkled and slid into some velvety soft lavender pajamas. Francis sat quietly at the door and they both gave a start when the doorbell chimed.

They hurried downstairs to find Moira with an armload of pizza. Jasmine was relieved to find that Moira had also changed into her pajamas. Of course, hers were a bit more stylish, she wore a neon pink satin gown and a full black robe. It was quite glamorous, especially for Merritt

"You always look like a rock star. Here let me help you." Jasmine collected a stack of pizza boxes from her friend. Moira twirled and they both laughed.

"I like to feel like a rock star. Take those to the coffee table in there, will you?" she gestured toward the sitting room. "I'll grab us some wine. Red goes with pizza, right?" Moira giggled as she disappeared toward the kitchen.

Jasmine deposited the pizzas on an oversized white coffee table. Jasmine remembered this room very differently. Where it had once been all oak woodwork and red paint, it was now bright white and full of life. Where there used to be stately leather couches and a recliner, there was a dramatic oversized purple couch and matching chair. There were houseplants in pots all over and several hanging plants, too. The untouched woodwork even seemed brighter without the dark paint framing it.

Moira reappeared with two bottles of wine, two glasses, some plates, and napkins.

"Two bottles, hm?" Jasmine scolded playfully.

"Mhm, one for each of us." Moira joked. She set the table, as it were, and turned on the tv, leaving the volume low. They helped themselves to hearty slices of Chicago-style pizza and Moira poured them each some wine.

Jasmine settled into the oversized armchair and Moira lounged on the couch. Jasmine gobbled up her pizza and was considering a second slice when she realized the painting behind Moira was Moira, posed almost as she was sitting currently.

"Oh wow, that's you!" she said with surprise.

"Hm? Oh, yes. Moira caught onto what had surprised her friend. It was a primitive style painting, with more muted colors than the others Jasmine had seen tonight, but it was clearly Moira and beautifully painted. "I dated a painter for a while, too. Christof. He did a couple of the paintings in the study, too."

"Oh, it's just lovely, Moira. I have to say I just love what you've done with the space here. It's still the same house. But it's not." Jasmine sipped some wine.

"Well, that was my intention, honestly. I wanted to honor my parents but make the place mine, too.

"I love it. Your style is so unique. I saw the studio upstairs, are you designing, or?" Jasmine inquired.

"Oh, I'm just starting to. So far I've just made myself a few things and tailored a few pieces for customers. I'd love to create a line, though." Moira ran her hand through her hair.

"You've got the style for it. Your designs would be 100% original." Jasmine said, sincerely. She decided to go in for that second piece.

"I hope you're right, I'm hoping to design a collection next year." Moira simply beamed discussing her passion. "Maybe you'll model for me? You're exactly the right size for it."

"I don't know about that. I mean I'd be happy to, but you'll have to let everything out if I eat another bite." They laughed together and Jasmine sank back into the plush chair.

They gabbed about Moira's past boyfriends and the years she spent studying in Europe before she had settled down back home. Moira regaled Jasmine with stories of fashion shows and five-star restaurants, and they laughed about the eccentric designers she'd worked under until Jasmine's sides ached.

After dinner, they collected up the boxes and Jasmine helped Moira put leftovers away. Francis was delighted to have a few bits of pizza crust in exchange for a handshake. His tricks seemed to be a huge hit everywhere Jasmine took him. She decided they would stop by the rescue booths at the festival fair on Saturday, maybe they could boost adoptions together.

"Say, you think you could try something on for me?" Moira pulled Jasmine away from her thoughts.

“Uhm. Sure.” Jasmine replied with some trepidation. She wasn’t sure what she’d gotten herself into but she followed Moira upstairs to the sewing room. The space was even brighter than the sitting room. Here, though, the art was minimal. Instead, the walls were lined with idea boards, full of magazine clippings and Moira’s sketches. Endless colored reams of fabric were stacked and strewn about, and a few finished pieces hung on a rack near the window.

Moira produced an elegant intense sunset yellow. It seemed to be strapless. Moira stuck out a bottom lip.

“Please? I’ve been dying to see it on someone and it’s far too small for me.” She handed the dress over. Moira’s curves were a bit ampler than her own. She decided to acquiesce and turned around to slide out of her pajamas. Moira prattled on about the other dresses she was working on before zipping her into the impressive gown. Jasmine swirled around.

“Oh my god. Stunning. You may have missed your calling, Jazz. Have a look.” She gestured to a set of full-length mirrors in the corner. Jasmine moved toward them, noticing how the dress seemed to float with her steps.

“Oh wow. Moira this is beautiful. I’ve never seen anything like it.” The bodice framed her waistline without constricting her and even without straps, the dress wasn’t too revealing. The skirt was huge. It reminded Jasmine of princesses or old fashioned prom gowns. She could easily see it on a celebrity on a red carpet. She was still admiring the dress when she heard her phone ringing in the next room. She had to lift the skirt to run in it, but she scurried down the hall, a flight of golden skirts and ebony curls.

She got to the phone just in time. It was Eric but he was making a video call. She slid the icon to accept.

“Hi beautiful!” he exclaimed. He got a look at her and chuckled. “Did I interrupt a run? You seem out of breath.”

“Oh, no. I was just modeling a dress for Moira. Jasmine tipped the phone up to get more of herself in the frame and gave a little twirl. Eric chuckled again.

"Looks great on you. Do you have a date to homecoming?" He joked.

"Maaaaybe," Jasmine teased. "What are you up to?" Eric flipped to his other camera, revealing a barn and what Jasmine thought to be goats. He flipped it back.

"Fall kids. I think maybe five before the night is out. I just wanted to make sure you're okay tonight. You could come down here if you like, but it looks like you're busy, huh?"

"Yes, I'm staying at Moira's tonight. She didn't want me to be alone, but I'm having the greatest time." Jasmine smiled at him. He was so handsome there in his element.

"I'm happy to hear it. I agree with her, too. Well, have fun, sweetheart. Maybe text me if you're not too busy at the ball with Prince Charming." He laughed again.

"Oh, he knows I've already got a date. Talk to you later." As she set her phone back down she felt herself grinning. Her Prince Charming hung out in straw piles with goats while they were kidding. She didn't think she'd want it any other way. She floated back to the sewing room and found Moira at the top of the stairs.

"I'm so sorry for running around in your dress!" Jasmine offered.

"What nonsense. Dresses are meant to be worn. It wouldn't do me much good if you couldn't run around or flirt with sexy farm vets in it." Moira gave a wink. "I wonder if you could stand here on the stairs for a photo? I can add it to my portfolio."

"Oh, okay." Jasmine hesitated.

"You look amazing Jazz, I promise," Moira assured.

Jasmine tried to believe her. She'd already spent enough time in front of a camera today. Still, she tried to pose naturally. Moira pushed a large golden fake flower into the crown of her hair and fussed with the skirt of the dress. When it was lying just so, she went down several steps and snapped several shots with her phone, prompting Jasmine to turn her head or raise her chin. When she was satisfied she had her shot she motioned for Jasmine to move.

Jasmine got changed and hung the gown back on the rack. It was beautiful but she was happy to get back into her comfortable pajamas and find her way back to the oversized chair downstairs. Moira was opening the second bottle of wine when she arrived.

"Oh Jazz, look!" Moira handed her phone over. "You really could model. I mean just look at you! And that's without fancy lighting and makeup."

Jasmine took in the photos. She had to admit, they were lovely. She was making a silly face in a couple, but overall the way the color of the dress flattered her russet skin tone and the way the dress lay in soft folds over the stairs was artful. It looked a little like pictures she'd seen in fashion magazines.

"Well, perhaps I'll model some more for you sometime. That was fun." She smiled and took the proffered glass of wine in exchange for Moira's phone.

"If you don't mind I'm going to put this on my website. But I'll wait until…." Moira trailed off.

"Wait until, what?" Jasmine prompted.

"Well, I was going to say I'll wait until they arrest whoever's been threatening you." A shadow fell across Moira's face.

"Oh, I guess that's a good idea," Jasmine said calmly.

"Why do I feel like the rest of us are more worried about those threats than you are?" Moira curled back up on her perch.

"I mean. I'm worried, too. But, frankly, I don't think they're going to follow through, they just want me to stop looking into Lily's murder." Jasmine sipped her wine. "I'll be as careful as I can be but I refuse to live my life in fear."

"You're braver than I. If someone threatened my life I'd probably be on a plane to Milan right now." Moira laughed and Jasmine was relieved to see her friend brighten back up. "That's always an option, you know. Say the word and I will whisk you away from the dangers of Merritt Valley."

Jasmine giggled. It was just after ten pm and the local news was coming on. Moira leaned in to turn up the volume. A stuffy looking anchorman explained that Sam Day had been brought to the station that afternoon, and they showed some clips of him being escorted into a police car and then some shots of him at the station in city hall. There was a clip of Detective Williams trying to brush off the reporters and refusing to call Sam a primary suspect.

A commercial break cut off the detective, and when KBRT news returned, Jasmine's smiling face greeted the audience. Off-screen, Jasmine hid her blushing cheeks behind her hands. She watched the interview through parted fingers. The interview went well enough and Francis was simply adorable. Still, Jasmine hoped she wouldn't have to do that again any time soon.

Moira clicked her tongue. "You're so silly Jazz. I know you're not shy and the camera loves you."

"Well thank you but that's a one-sided romance. I just hate being on tv. You do the next fluff piece for Nancy, okay?" She laughed. "I don't know about you, but I'm beat. I think I'll walk Francis and hit the sheets."

"Mm. Sleep sounds divine." Moira stretched and turned things off before wandering out with her wine glass. "Night Jazz, come get me if you hear any bumps in the night."

"I will, goodnight Moira." Jasmine slipped her leather coat on over her PJs and stepped into her boots. She and Francis stepped out into the cool night air. While they walked the sidewalk in Moira's upscale neighborhood, Jasmine couldn't help but look over her shoulder for dark figures in hoods.

She was happy to be back safely within the walls of Moira's stately brick manor. She and Francis meandered up to bed. She sank blissfully into the plush down bedding and checked her phone. There were several texts congratulating her on the news piece, and a picture message from Eric. There he was, cradling a brand new baby goat in one arm. It said simply.

"Goodnight gorgeous."

"Goodnight handsome." She replied. She sank back into the pillows and tried to sleep. It had been such a long, full day. A news interview, a high-speed chase, an interlude with a probable killer. Okay, maybe it had been a low speed chase. Either way, it had been one of the most eventful days Jasmine had seen in years. The evening had been full, too. Modeling that gown had been fun. She sighed and decided to make tomorrow more low-key. Before she could decide how, she drifted off into a deep and well-earned slumber.

CHAPTER TWELVE

Six am Wednesday, October 10th Jasmine's alarm drew her out of dreamless sleep. She stretched and looked around, disoriented for a moment. It was always kind of strange to wake up in an unfamiliar place. She made the bed and turned on the shower in the guest bath. After a lingering hot shower, she got dressed simply, cream colored sweater, fitted khakis, and thick knit socks. She'd put her boots on later.

Downstairs she found Moira's bedroom door still shut. She imagined her friend must still be sleeping. She tried to keep the noise down as she poked around for breakfast. She made some toast with strawberry jam and fiddled with the coffee pot. By the time she had found a quiet place to read the news for the day and enjoy her breakfast with Francis at her side, she could hear Moira stirring in the back bedroom.

Jasmine sent an email to Claire and the rest of the staff at the clinic to let them know she'd be out for the day. She never took time off but she thought being threatened by a killer was as good a reason as any. She read local and national news and enjoyed her coffee. Nearly an hour passed before Moira emerged.

"Good morning babe!" Moira chimed. She grabbed a travel cup of coffee and a granola bar.

"No time for breakfast, this morning?" Jasmine asked.

"Oh, I wish! But we were so busy yesterday I needed to stock and tidy up before we opened. So busy during the festival!" Moira was in a flurry grabbing things and stuffing them into an oversized rainbow leopard print bag.

"We have the opposite issue at the clinic. I'm taking a couple of days off." Jasmine mentioned.

"Oh good! You never take time off. Say, make yourself at home, please. Help yourself to whatever, come and go as you please. You have your key, right?" she asked and Jasmine nodded. "Good. I'll be back here around the same time tonight. Try and enjoy your day off!" Moira made a kissy face and swept out of the room.

A whole day to herself. Jasmine wasn't sure what on earth to do. Normally with an unexpected free day, she would clean her house or run errands. Neither of those would be good options today. The shops would all be too crowded to enjoy errands and she thought it best to avoid her house for a couple of days. If mystery hoodie was leaving her creepy poems, well, they'd just have to wait.

However, Jasmine supposed she could devote some of this free time putting a name and face to the hoodie.

Jasmine ran upstairs to fetch the black ledger of special orders from Moira's boutique. She plopped the book on the coffee table and fetched another cup. Francis curled up under the big table and she began to scan the book as she had yesterday. It was nearly 8 am when she came across a name that caught her attention. Molly Stephens. She was the other actress on Detective Williams's list. If Jasmine remembered right, Molly had a clear criminal history but had said some suggestive things to Sam Day on more than one occasion.

Jasmine ran her finger along the line with Molly's name… what had she ordered? A vintage style vanity set! It was nearly a year ago, she'd ordered the set in November 2017. The record didn't mention what the brush was made of, but Jasmine felt like this was an important break in this case. She grabbed her phone and looked up Molly Stephen's address. She was just about to zip up her boots and go say hello when her phone rang.

"Jasmine Cline," Jasmine answered.

"Hi, this is Detective Williams."

"Oh hello, Detective."

"Good morning. I wondered if we could meet later. Informally, no fingerprints, I promise." Jasmine could swear Cassandra Williams was trying to make a joke.

"Uhm, sure. What time? You want me to come down to the station?" Jasmine inquired.

"No no, maybe around noon? We can grab some lunch." Williams offered. Jasmine considered for a moment. Molly Stephens lived a few miles from the old diner. If they met there, Jasmine would already be in the neighborhood.

"Hum, maybe the old diner? You know, near the highway?" Jasmine never could remember the name of that place.

"Good Old Days? Sure. I'll see you there." Williams hung up without giving Jasmine time to reply. Quick and to the point, Jasmine thought. It occurred to her she shouldn't leave Francis at Moira's alone and she didn't want to leave him in the Jeep for extended periods. She shot off a quick text to her mother, Donna Cline.

"Hey mom, can I drop Francis off with you today?"

"Sure. You still owe me a coffee date! - mom." She had forgotten all about coffee with mom. Well, she'd make it up to her. First, she had a murder to solve.

Jasmine took the highway to the old part of town. There were a series of houses, a small school, and a couple of boarding houses that dated back to the early 1900s when Merritt Valley was a new town. Jasmine thought the school had been converted into apartments or office space now, but she so rarely needed to come to this area of town she couldn't be sure.

Molly Stephens was renting a room in one of the old boarding houses. Jasmine parked out front and once inside the foyer, scanned the mailboxes, and found that Molly was in apartment 4, on the second floor. She didn't want to buzz in, Molly had no reason to let her up. It would be harder to say no, face to face. The main entrance was locked, and Jasmine was considering her options when a sweet older lady opened the door for her.

"Good morning!" Jasmine said brightly.

"Morning dear." The woman smiled. Jasmine ran up the stairs and found the door to number four, complete with a welcome mat and a fall-themed wreath hanging from the door.

Jasmine swallowed heavily and tapped on the door. She waited a moment and just as she was about to reach out and knock again, she heard someone moving on the other side of the door.

It creaked open to reveal a full-figured petite woman in her late twenties. She had a kind face, pale blue eyes, and mousy brown hair. She was a bit disheveled and purple shadows had formed below her eyes.

"I...um. Hello." Molly seemed confused to see Jasmine.

"Good morning. Sorry to bother you, but I'm Jasmine Cline. I - I was a friend of Lily Day's." Jasmine explained. "I wondered if I could talk to you for a moment."

Molly still looked confused, but stepped out of the door and gestured for Jasmine to come in.

"I recognize you, weren't you on the news last night?" Molly asked.

"Oh yeah, I was. Although I think Francis played the leading role." Jasmine smiled.

"He kind of did, huh? He's super cute. Please come on in, have a seat." Molly offered. "So what was it you wanted to talk about?" Jasmine swallowed again. Interviewing suspects was new territory for her, and honestly, she wasn't entirely sure she should be. But she had to follow her hunch. She decided honesty was the best option here.

"Well, you see. Lily Day may have died because she was allergic to horses." Jasmine began.

"Horses? At the theater?" Molly interrupted.

"Well you know, not an actual horse, but perhaps a makeup or hairbrush. You know, many of them are made with horsehair, especially antiques." Jasmine continued.

"Oh yeah, you know, I had a brush like that. It was part of a set." Molly interjected.

Jasmine was taken off guard. That was easier than she thought. "Had? May I ask what happened to it?"

"Oh, it went missing after the show last spring. We did Four Weddings and an Elvis. It was hilarious. Did you see it?" she asked. Jasmine shook her head. "Oh, well, it was a great show. Sam played Elvis. Anyhow lots of the ladies have these pretty vanity sets for their mirrors in the dressing rooms. You know, to go with their makeup and stuff. People give them as gifts a lot. I always wanted one but no one ever gifted me one so last year I just got my own." Molly went on. Jasmine was relieved to find Molly so forthcoming.

"But something happened to it?" Jasmine prodded.

"Yeah. After the final show, there's usually a cast party. Half my set went missing, the brush and the comb. I still have the handheld mirror and the mirror tray you put them all on, you know? I thought maybe someone just packed them by mistake. It's real rare for people to steal from their castmates but they never did turn back up." Molly finished.

"Well, that's too bad. I wonder where they got to. That's really all I wanted to ask you about." Jasmine was about to stand up when Molly gasped.

"Geez, you don't think maybe Lily ended up with my brush do ya, Miss Cline? That would be so awful." Molly looked crestfallen.

"I think it may be a possibility," Jasmine answered honestly. "I'm sure we'll all know soon enough, what really happened." Molly seemed sweet and endearing, but Jasmine hadn't forgotten that the girl was a seasoned actress. "I guess I better get going. May I use your restroom? I think I had too much coffee this morning."

"Oh sure. It's at the end of the hall." Molly said with a point. Jasmine found the restroom easily enough. She was hoping to see that vanity set on the counter, but it was just a pedestal sink. No space for pretty mirror trays. Jasmine heard a phone ring, and while she couldn't make out the conversation, she could hear that Molly was quite involved in a conversation.

Jasmine took the opportunity to sneak out of the bathroom and peek into the bedroom. Molly wasn't going to win any housekeeping awards. There were clothes strewn about and a growing pile of laundry on the floor. But there, among the dust and discarded tissues, was the remains of a lovely vanity set. Just the large oval mirror, with the smaller handheld mirror lying face down on it. Jasmine swiftly snapped a shot of the mirror and hurried back to the front room.

She nodded to Molly, who was still on the phone. "Hey hold on," She said into her cell. "Oh hey, did you need anything else, Doc?" Molly asked.

"No, no. I'll just see myself out. Take care, Molly." Jasmine made her way out of the modest apartment and Molly was back to laughing with her friend before she'd shut the door behind her.

Jasmine drove straight to the diner. She was quite early for her lunch with Detective Williams. She took a seat at a booth and ordered some hot tea. She ruminated over her conversation with Molly Stephens. Molly gave off a casual innocence. She even played a bit dumb. Jasmine couldn't help to wonder how much of that was her true personality, and how much was play-acting. Molly had been in dozens of productions, it was possible she took acting very seriously.

Common people lied about crimes they committed every single day. Surely, a decent actress could lie about their part in a murder. But there was something else. Jasmine couldn't deny that the person in the dark hoodie was rather slight in all ways. Slim, and shorter than herself. The first time she'd seen them in their dark raincoat, they'd been running. Molly was not a slim girl and Jasmine very much doubted that running was among her hobbies.

Jasmine guessed maybe Molly could be working with someone else if she was involved at all. All this intrigue was making Jasmine rather suspicious of everyone, but Molly not have been lying at all. Maybe her only involvement had been losing her horsehair brush. She didn't know why but Jasmine felt pretty certain that hairbrush was the one used to kill Lily Day.

But who had stolen it?

Jasmine had nearly finished the entire pot of tea when Detective Williams arrived. She was early too, but only by a few minutes. The Detective was back in her usual work clothes, black slacks, white button-up, utility belt, and today a black jacket. She almost smiled when she noticed Jasmine already sitting at a booth.

"Well well, you're rather punctual, Doctor," Williams said as she took the seat opposite Jasmine.

"Jasmine, please. And yes, I do try to be early as often as possible. How's your day?"

"It's been eventful. There have been quite a few developments on the case." Williams stated flatly.

"Oh? What sort of developments?" Jasmine asked. A waitress interrupted with menus and they both glanced over them.

"Yes, I'll get into it after we order. How's your day been?" Williams inquired.

"It's also been eventful. I took the day off and I have some developments of my own."

Detective Williams gave her a quizzical look and the waitress returned. Jasmine ordered that burger and fries she'd been thinking about yesterday. Williams ordered a grilled chicken wrap, salad instead of fries.

"Somehow I didn't imagine you as a burger and fries person," Williams commented after their waitress vanished with their orders.

"Once in a while, but honestly I love good food, that's why I run so much. Well, one of the reasons."

"What are the other reasons?" Williams seemed to be making small talk.

"Oh, running clears my head. It helps me stay focused and helps me to sleep soundly at night." Jasmine was hoping to get in a run later today.

"I like running for all those reasons, too. But mostly I run so I can catch bad guys when I need to." Williams responded with a serious tone.

"I guess that's a necessity. Say, what kind of developments did you have in the case?" Jasmine was dying to know.

"Well," Detective Williams gave the diner a sweeping once over. It was nearly empty. All the action was happening downtown. She continued, "that EpiPen you found was expired."

"But, they still work after the expiration date, generally." Jasmine considered aloud.

"Yes, they do. This means that fact alone doesn't eliminate Sam as a suspect. It does, however, mean that Lily May have had a newer one, and tossed that one, herself."

"Oh, I guess that's true. Then that would leave us where we started. The killer would have had to dispose of the EpiPen Lily kept on her, probably on that same night." Jasmine finished.

"Yes that would leave *us* right where we started," Detective Williams quipped. "You do know you're not an investigator. Right?"

"Well of course I know that." Jasmine resisted the urge to roll her eyes. The waitress appeared with their food and she dug right in. After pizza and such last night, maybe she should have had a wrap or a salad, herself. But as she bit into that burger, any sense of regret faded away.

"You said that you had a development, yourself. Can you tell me about that?" Williams chomped into her wrap. It looked rather tasty.

"Sure. I… I went to see Molly Stephens this morning." Jasmine swallowed her nerves.

"You what? What would possess you to go see a person of interest, yourself? Alone?" The Detective sounded both concerned and annoyed.

"Well, you'll remember I thought Lily's allergy may have been triggered by a hairbrush? I know the brush that was found on her dressing table turned out to be acrylic. I thought maybe someone switched brushes and then switched them back after." Jasmine explained.

"You mean to say, someone knew Lily was allergic to horses. Got a horsehair brush that looked like her fancy silver-plated brush, made a switch, and then casually put the acrylic brush back, in the middle of an investigation. After having stolen her EpiPen, of course. And now they're hiding the murder weapon.... A hairbrush." Williams scoffed. "You realize how convoluted all that sounds. Why would they go through all that trouble? Why wouldn't they just... shoot her?"

"Well, we don't all wear pistols, Detective. But think about it. Whoever killed Lily put a lot of work into not getting caught. An allergy could have just been written off as accidental death. No investigation. I mean, you didn't even open a homicide investigation for 3 days. They were trying to get away with murder, and they almost did." Jasmine finished with passionate resolve.

The Detective sat back in the booth and took a deep breath.

"Okay. You've got a solid point." Williams conceded. "But what does any of this have to do with Molly Stephens?"

"Sam ordered Lily's vanity set from Blackbird. You know, that clothing store on Grand Avenue. He special ordered it because they're so often made with horsehair, and he wanted to be sure Lily could use his gift. So, I thought maybe the killer ordered theirs from Blackbird, too. I went through their special orders for the last couple of years, and only one other person had ordered a vintage look vanity set." Jasmine took a long drink of water.

"Molly Stephens." The Detective finished for her.

"Molly Stephens." Jasmine agreed. "So I paid her a visit."

"And what did you discover upon this visit?" Williams inquired.

"I discovered that those vanity sets are popular with our local theater ladies. Molly wanted one and ordered it herself. And half of it is missing."

"Missing?"

"Molly's story was that half her set was stolen, or misplaced, during the cast party for last spring's play. Something about Elvis."

"But that could just be a story," Williams suggested.

"Exactly. I did get a shot of what's left of her set." Jasmine pulled up the photo for the Detective.

"Send me the shot, please." Williams requested.

"Sure." Jasmine took care of sending the photo and picked at her fries. "Oh, there's something else."

"What's that?" Williams said between bites of her lunch.

"Even if she is involved in Lily's death, Molly isn't the person in the dark hoodie."

"She's not?" Williams asked.

"No, she's a bit. Curvier, than mystery hoodie." Jasmine said delicately.

"Ah. Yes, the figure in the photo looks quite slender." Williams set her napkin down. "About that. We found out who that car is registered to. Mark Fitzgerald."

"Mark? The maintenance guy from the theater?" Jasmine was shocked.

"The one and the same." Williams responded.

"Mark is much larger than mystery hoodie. And male." Jasmine stated the obvious.

"Curious, isn't it?" Williams asked, rhetorically. "Something else is curious if you wanted to get away with murder, why would you leave handwritten notes to lead authorities right to you? You're right that they may have gotten away with this if it weren't for the threats in those notes."

"Well, I haven't worked out that part yet," Jasmine answered frankly. "Maybe they figured no one would ever see the notes. I mean, didn't one note say something about being his love, and they'd have a chance with Lily out of the way? Maybe they thought Sam would fall into their arms the moment his wife was gone."

"I guess that's a possibility." The waitress appeared with their bills and cleared some empty plates. "Say, Jasmine, I asked you to lunch rather than the station for a reason. I appreciate your insight and I'd be lying if I said that you haven't been instrumental in this case. But I need you to understand that this work is dangerous, especially if you're working alone and without training."

"I know," Jasmine said with sincerity.

"Please be careful. If you're going to go visit someone you think may have had a part in *murder* call me. Okay?"

"Okay. I will." Jasmine almost said, "I promise," but stopped short.

"Very good." I'll call you if I learn anything. Do the same?" Jasmine nodded. "Great. I've got to get back. Stay safe." Detective Williams dropped some cash with her bill and left.

Jasmine took care of her bill as well and collected her things. She decided to take the Detective's advice, at least for today. She wouldn't go snooping around anymore suspects. At least not today.

Instead, she decided to have a long run and maybe after, a bath in that big clawfoot tub back at Moira's. She was glad she'd brought her running gear. She took the highway up to the same trail she and Eric had hiked only a few days ago. They had nice shower stalls at Laurentian Park since the park also had a campground. Jasmine got changed quickly. When she hit the trail, she opted for soft ambient music. She took a slower steady pace since she'd just eaten and this was a longer trail.

Jasmine loved this trail. The tall trees lent a feeling of adventure to the run and their full pine scent filled her lungs and surrounded her. The terrain was challenging enough to keep it interesting without being too hard. She would have to come up here to run a few more times before winter hit,

The place reminded her of that day with Eric. Had it only been a few days since their first date? She felt like they'd fallen into things so easily. She hoped he felt the same. She paused at a lookout to stretch and enjoy the view. This was another side of the valley. From here the changing leaves seemed so distant, her view was dominated by endless emerald pines with flashes of white aspens. She turned so the view was behind her and snapped a selfie.

"Thinking of you." she captioned the photo and sent it to Eric. She pocketed her phone and got back into her steady groove. She'd have to ask him to come to the fair with her this weekend. Aside from all the baked goodies, the Festival Fair was Jasmine's favorite part of Festival of Leaves. There would be a huge open farmer's market, and farmers showing animals of all kinds. In the evening local bands would play, and some local brew houses would debut their autumn and winter beers.

Jasmine was imagining slow dancing on a wooden dance floor surrounded by carnival lights and other happy couples. Oh, she hoped he could dance. Jasmine chuckled to herself. She reached the end of the trail and could see her Jeep in the lot. Her phone rang and stirred her out of her daydream. She was delighted to see who it was.

"Hi!" She greeted Eric happily.

"Hey, beautiful. How's your run?"

“It was great. I was just thinking about you,” she replied.

“You did mention that. Anything good?” he asked with a grin.

“Everything good. Say Eric, can you dance?”

“I can, if the occasion calls for it. How come? Did Prince Charming ditch you for the ball?” Eric joked.

“Maybe he did. If the occasion calls for it, huh? What if the occasion is the Festival Fair, Saturday?”

“I think that could be arranged.” he chuckled. “I probably don’t need a suit for that sort of dancing, do I?”

“No, you certainly don’t. And I’m afraid I won’t be in a ball gown.” Jasmine laughed.

“Aw, that’s too bad. But you’ll look beautiful no matter what.” Eric always knew just what to say to make her blush.

“Well, it’s a date then,” she announced.

“It’s a date.” Eric agreed.

She was grinning like a schoolgirl by the time they hung up and she got back into her Jeep. The skies were turning as they had when she and Eric had stopped up here. Maybe her visits to the Laurentian trails somehow triggered rain. By the time she arrived at Moira's, the sky was quite dark though the rain hadn't started. Jasmine grabbed her bag and went straight up to her room. She was pleased to discover that, though the tub looked antique, maybe original to the house, the fixtures looked brand new. She lit a couple of candles and slipped into the deep old tub.

Jasmine had always loved big tubs like this one. She allowed all her muscles to fully relax in the steaming water and she felt like any tension she'd been carrying just floated away. She heard thunder in the distance. She was so relaxed when she got out of that bath all she just slipped into a simple strappy nightdress and then into the sheets. She fell into a dreamy sleep just as fast as her head touched the pillow.

She woke to the sounds of Latin music floating up from the kitchen. She sat up in the dark and stretched. As she inhaled, Jasmine noticed the scents of food cooking but she couldn't recognize what. Jasmine's head spun. She was still sleepy and if she sank back down into the blankets she could easily sleep 8 more hours. She was deeply tempted to do just that.

Still, she was a guest and she adored Moira's company. She pulled a sweater over her nightdress and tugged into some leggings. She pulled on some cozy wool socks and headed downstairs. She paused a moment. She felt like she was forgetting something. Francis. He was safe with her mother but she found she missed the pooch. She sighed and opened the door to the kitchen.

She found Moira cooking and dancing to music she'd never heard before. Moira called out, "Hey babe!" and continued her dancing. Jasmine decided to be useful and set out some place settings on the island in the kitchen, rather than in the formal dining room. Moira smiled broadly and turned down the music.

"I found you snoozing when I got home so I thought I'd make you some Caribbean food." Moira was in a dazzling mood.

"It smells amazing. I can't say I've ever had Caribbean food." Jasmine admitted.

"Well, good, then you won't know if I killed these recipes or not." Moira laughed and placed bowls of delicious looking foods out on the island. Jasmine didn't recognize any of them. Moira took a large pitcher of water with lemons and mint leaves in it from the fridge and added it to the spread.

"This is chicken curry, coconut rice, doubles, and some plantain." Moira pointed to each dish. Jasmine scooped up small amounts of each and poured herself a large glass of water. She took trepidatious bites of each. Though the flavors were unfamiliar they were all delicious. She especially enjoyed the coconut rice which seemed to simply be rice cooked in coconut milk. It was just sweet enough and she was pleased to have some lighter fare.

Moira told Jasmine all about her day at the shop and all the tourists who came through the doors. She also told her how she learned to cook Caribbean food while in France. Moira's life seemed so exotic to Jasmine, she was pleased to have a friend who had seen and tasted and felt so much of the world.

"So you've heard all about my day. How was yours? And spur of the moment dates?" Moira raised her eyebrows suggestively and Jasmine laughed.

"Unfortunately not today. But we did set a date for Saturday." Jasmine smiled at the thought of it. She knew she'd be daydreaming of that dance until it happened.

"Ooo. I'm going to be there too, one of the bands bought their outfits at the shop. Anything else exciting happen?" Moira prodded.

"Well, I found someone who ordered a vanity set from you, and went to see her."

"Who was it?" Moira asked.

"Molly Stephens," Jasmine replied and Moira shrugged. "The brush was horsehair, but doesn't have it anymore she claims it was stolen at the theater last spring."

“So anyone could have it,” Moira mentioned.

“Exactly. I also had lunch with Detective Williams.” Jasmine finished her glass of water and poured another. That unexpected nap left her parched.

“How was that?”

“Better than I thought it was going to be. She hasn’t made much progress on the case but it was good to discuss it all with her.”

“I hope she starts to make progress, and soon.” Moira wasn’t as patient as Jasmine. Jasmine nodded and set her fork down.

“You want some help cleaning up?” she asked.

“No no, I’ve got this. Are you okay babe?” Moira asked in response.

“Oh, I’m fine. Great really, I had a nice run and the most wonderful bath earlier. I’m going to steal your bathtub.” she chuckled. “I’m just so tired.”

“You’ve had a crazy few days. Go on back to bed.” Moira squeezed her shoulder.

“You know, I think I will. Goodnight, and thanks for dinner, it was so lovely.”

“Goodnight Jazz.” Moira smiled and started to clean up after their lovely meal.

Jasmine felt heavy on her way up the stairs. It had been a lovely meal and a nice chat with her friend, but she was deeply relieved to sink back into the plush bed in the guestroom. She looked at her phone only long enough to see a goodnight message from Eric and send him a short, “Night, handsome,” in return.

She nuzzled into the pillows and sank into a contented sleep.

CHAPTER THIRTEEN

Jasmine opened her eyes Thursday morning before her alarm. She stretched and took a deep breath. She felt more rested than she had in ages. She took her time styling her hair and getting ready. Today she wore a soft rose-colored tunic over faux leather leggings. She was pretty sure she'd purchased those leggings at Moira's shop, Blackbird.

The reason for her visit was unfortunate but Jasmine was grateful to reconnect with her old friend. She hoped they would spend more time together once this whole mess was sorted out. She hoped that was very soon.

Jasmine found her way downstairs. She assumed Moira would still be in her room. She was right. Jasmine made coffee and poured some in a travel mug for her friend. She poured herself a cup and peeked in the cupboards for something that looked like breakfast. Moira's taste in food was so different from her own, she hardly recognized most of the contents of Moira's cupboards. She found a fruit and cereal bar and settled in with her coffee.

Jasmine checked her schedule online. Since their clinic was mobile, often Jasmine's days began in the home of a client, rather than at the office. Not today, however. Not a single appointment. The Festival of Leaves was wonderful, but it was just awful for business.

Jasmine tapped out a text to Brian and the other interns to see anyone needed to work on practicals. A couple of them answered yes, so at least she could spend some time teaching today.

Moira emerged from her room just after 7 am.

"Good morning Jazz! Nice to see you up and about, you had me worried last night." Moira started to look for a coffee cup and was pleasantly surprised to find one filled and ready to go.

"Oh, nothing to worry about. The run and the hot bath just tired me out, is all," she replied.

"Still, nice to see you awake at the crack of dawn." Moira chuckled. "I'm off. See you tonight?"

"See you tonight," Jasmine called after Moira who buzzed out of the house in her hurried way. Jasmine lingered over her coffee. With no appointments scheduled, there would be no charts to go over before her day normally began at 8 am.

Jasmine pulled into the parking lot five minutes before 8. She spent time going over vaccination procedures and suturing with the interns. They spent the morning working hard and Jasmine thought they all had good hands and great potential. The lesson was over by lunch. Claire appeared just after noon with a couple of sandwiches.

"When do they release the dates for the Festival of Leaves?" Claire asked wearily.

"Oh, I think it's going on right now." Jasmine joked.

"I know that." Claire scoffed playfully. "I mean next for next year."

"I think it's always the second week of October. What makes you ask?" Jasmine inquired.

"I'm going to book a vacation." Claire was exasperated but she wasn't kidding. Neither she nor Jasmine had a knack for waiting around.

"Where will you go?" Jasmine wondered aloud.

"Maybe Hawaii. I've never been." Claire replied.

“Oh, then you must go. It’s so beautiful. It was my favorite vacation.” Jasmine didn’t mention it was also her only big vacation. She had always been so preoccupied with her studies, there hadn’t been much time for travel. Her mother Donna had insisted on the trip to Hawaii when she finished her graduate degree.

“I think I’ll save a bit on the trip if I book so far out. I just can’t sit around here, it's driving me mad.” Claire ran a tense hand through her thick red hair.

“Well, you don’t have to wait around. I’ll stick around the office this afternoon.” Jasmine offered.

“Are you sure? That would be nice. I could work on my house. Maybe finish the guest bath.” Claire had purchased a small house in Merritt Valley around the same time that Jasmine bought hers. Claire’s house was more of a fixer-upper and had been in a perpetual state of remodeling since they both moved to the small town.

“Of course I’m sure.” Jasmine smiled. Claire got up, she seemed more at ease than she had when she sat down.

“Thanks, Jazz,” she mumbled and ambled off.

Jasmine enjoyed her sandwich. Brian popped his head in shortly after Claire left.

“What’s up Brian?” Jasmine asked.

“Would you mind running some terms with me?” he asked.

“I dunno, I’m pretty busy, as you can see.” Jasmine joked. “Come on in.”

So she spent the afternoon playing study partner to a bright young veterinary intern. When he left at 4 pm, Jasmine thought he had a good handle on the modules they’d gone over together.

She wanted to work out but that run yesterday was plenty. Maybe she'd see if the yoga studio had an afternoon session. Jasmine ran out to her Jeep and grabbed her bag. She waved to Ellie on her way out the front door.

"Go ahead and lock up if I'm not back by 5!" She called over her shoulder.

The yoga studio was three blocks down. When Jasmine arrived there were plenty of people in the lobby but she couldn't tell if they were coming or going. She asked the young lady at the front desk.

"Is there a session this afternoon?"

"Yeah starts in 5 minutes. It's eleven dollars for the session."

"Sounds good," Jasmine handed over some cash.

"Sign here." The young woman passed over a form. "Changing room is down there." Jasmine signed her name and found the changing room. Once she was dressed for yoga she made her way back to the lobby. As she exited the changing room, Vicki Andrews was entering the front door. She was talking to the receptionist, so she didn't see Jasmine until she was standing right in front of her.

"Hello, Vicki, Jasmine said amicably.

"Um. Hi." Vicki shifted uneasily.

"I'm Jasmine, we met the other night at the playhouse." Jasmine stuck out her hand. Vicki just stared at her. "Ookay." She dropped her hand. Jasmine overheard the instructor getting ready to start the class. She turned and left Vicki with the receptionist.

Jasmine chose a space and rolled out her mat. As the instructor finished introductions, Jasmine caught sight of Vicki scurrying away from the studio as fast as her short legs would carry her. Before she could ruminate on how odd Vicki's behavior was, it was time to focus on her breath and start a sun salutation.

The session was lovely. Jasmine left the studio feeling refreshed and relaxed. It was a little after six when Jasmine arrived back at the Moira's. There were more people parked on the street than usual. When she got to the front door she found it unlocked and inside she found the house full of laughter and the scent of familiar foods cooking.

She followed the sounds and scents to the kitchen.

"Oh hi, baby!" Her mother Donna Cline was there, cooking alongside Moira. Claire was pulled up to the island with a glass of wine, chopping vegetables.

"Why, hi mom! Hey Claire. What are you two doing here?" Jasmine was pleasantly surprised.

"I hope you don't mind, Jazz. I thought a family-style supper might be good for all of us, and I've always wanted a cooking lesson from your mother." Moira piped in.

"Honey, everyone wants to know how to cook soul food!" Donna laughed.

"I think it's the best news I've ever heard," Jasmine replied. "Let me just get cleaned up."

Jasmine ran upstairs. She got washed up from yoga and put on some decent clothes. She smoothed her hair and hurried back down. Once back in the kitchen, she realized they were making chicken with cornbread stuffing. It was one of Jasmine's favorite meals. She pulled out her phone and adjusted until everyone was in the frame. She called out, "Hey everyone!" They all turned and she snapped the selfie.

Her mom clicked her tongue and laughed.

"How'd it turn out?" Claire asked.

"Looks great, see?" The picture had turned out surprisingly nice, though Moira looked a little shocked. Jasmine uploaded it immediately.

Donna was just wrapping up Moira's cooking lesson. Everything was nearly finished so Claire and Jasmine set the dining room table together.

"How's the bathroom coming?" Jasmine asked.

"It can wait." Claire smiled with a shrug.

Moira and Donna set out ample dishes full of greens, mashed potatoes, chicken, and stuffing. It looked like a feast. Moira opened some wine and everyone dished up. They shared Jasmine's favorite foods. The dining room was filled with stories and laughter. Donna told stories about cooking and then indulged Claire with some stories about Moira and Jasmine as girls, including the time they got grounded when they were 15, for trying to sneak out.

"They each lied, Jasmine told me she was staying here, and Moira told her mother she was staying at our place. I guess they forgot we had phones and could call each other." Donna laughed at the memory. She and Moira's mother Anna Randall had been great friends.

All the women spoke about their unusual week. The Festival had thrown all their usual routines for a loop, and of course, they talked about Lily's Day's mysterious death. As they began to clean up and pack the leftovers, Jasmine told them about her encounter with Vicki at the yoga studio this afternoon.

"You mean she just refused to shake your hand?" Claire asked when Jasmine had finished the story.

"Yes. She just stared at me like I have three heads. Then she got out of there so quickly." Jasmine explained.

"Like she's guilty of something," Moira added.

"Exactly." Claire agreed and the women exchanged knowing looks.

"I just don't like it. I can't believe Vicki would kill someone. I see her every day." Donna shook her head in disbelief.

"C'mon. Let's have some dessert." Moira changed the subject. She led Donna toward the sitting room.

"Gimme a hand?" Claire nudged Jasmine. "I made cheesecake."

Jasmine helped Claire carry out plates of cheesecake. The conversation steered away from murder and back to Moira's favorite topic; romance.

Claire believed she was terminally single, there weren't many eligible women in Merritt. As Jasmine knew, Moira was taking a break from dating. She called it a hiatus. They all wanted to know how things were going with Eric. Jasmine indulged them a little. She told them about their classic movie date, and how easily he had carried her the other night after they fell asleep on the couch. They gushed on about it and Jasmine squirmed.

"What about you, Donna?" Moira asked, "You think you'll ever date again?"

"Maybe. If the right man turns up." Donna grinned.

"Really?" Jasmine was surprised.

"Really, really. I loved your father dearly, but I'm still here and he's not." Donna answered frankly. Jasmine couldn't argue that.

"Maybe you'll meet a handsome stranger at the fair," Moira interjected.

"Oo maybe I will." Donna leaned back and they laughed and laughed.

After dessert, they all parted ways. While they were cleaning up dessert plates Jasmine paused to give Moira a squeeze.

"Thank you," she said. "Thanks for tonight. I needed that."

"It was my pleasure," Moira offered sincerely. "I needed it too. Wasn't it wonderful to have a houseful? Almost makes me want to get married." Moira chuckled.

"It was wonderful." Jasmine agreed.

When she finally settled into bed, Jasmine felt contented. Good food and time with her favorite people had been a balm to her heart. She snapped a sleepy selfie for Eric and sent him a sweet goodnight text before drifting off to a delicious sleep.

She had settled into the rhythm of the Randall house by the time Friday morning rolled around. Jasmine enjoyed a quick breakfast and cup of coffee while Moira got ready for her day. They left the house at the same time, Jasmine with Francis in tow. Jasmine noticed her mom Donna's SUV parked in front of the Lyric Theater. She'd have to stop and see her later, she'd missed a coffee date with her mom twice this week.

Jasmine parked in front of the animal clinic. Thanks to the Festival of Leaves, Merritt's annual autumn harvest festival, her appointment books had been woefully empty all week. She guessed today would be no different, and she wanted to be able to make a quick exit if there was nothing to do in the office. On her way into the building, Jasmine paused to admire the autumn display their office administrator Ellie had put together.

Ellie had gone with an apple theme, which Jasmine thought was a welcome departure from the pumpkins and scarecrows all over town. A small lit, leafless tree was decorated with shiny fake apples and a tiny ladder was also twined with twinkly lights. There were two small straw bales and half a dozen decorative baskets filled with real apples, along with a full burlap bag, staged to look like it had spilled apples all over the ground in the small window scene. Jasmine thought it was perfect.

The window display reminded her of her apple picking date with Eric Canton. She wondered what he'd done with the apples. There was a basket of them still on her kitchen counter but there were a couple of those burlap bags in the back of his pickup that Jasmine had completely forgotten about until now.

She got into work about 7 am and was surprised not to find Ellie at the front desk. Jasmine checked the record book herself and just as she'd thought, it was nearly empty. She had a ten am check-up with an aging poodle, and no other appointments. Jasmine deposited her bags in her office, left Francis to nap under the desk, and scrawled a note for Ellie to let her know she was getting coffee and would be back in time for her 10 am.

Jasmine popped back out into the crisp October air. The vendors were just beginning to set up shop and she could almost catch a glimpse of crews setting up the stands, lights, and signage for tomorrow's fair. Merritt Valley was a small town, their main street ended into open farmland, and it was in that space between street and field that the fair took place each year.

Rather than fight through the growing crowd at her favorite bakery and deli, The Muffin Man, Jasmine grabbed a couple of flavored lattes from a food truck parked across the street. She wandered down the street as the town began to wake up and begin the day. As she got up to the lovely old theater, she saw the maintenance man was sweeping away leaves and dust from the foyer.

"Good morning Mark!" She chimed.

"Oh good morning Jasmine. Here let me get the door for you." Mark was a quiet man, who seemed to keep to himself. She couldn't pinpoint his age but there was plenty of silver in his sandy brown hair. He was always polite to Jasmine. He opened one of the massive double doors.

“Say, Mark, I thought I saw your car the other day. A little silver Toyota at the grocery store? But I could have sworn a young lady was driving. Did you get a girlfriend without telling me?” Jasmine’s joke nearly made Mark blush and he laughed.

“Oh, no Miss Jasmine. I’m selling that car to a young lady. She only owes me one more payment then we’ll go transfer the title. You might know her, she was in the play here. Vicki Andrews. She’s my neighbor.” Mark explained.

“Oh, that’s so nice of you to work with her on payments. Thanks so much, Mark.” Jasmine smiled and Mark went back to his work. Jasmine shook her head. All roads seemed to lead to Vicki Andrews.

Most of the lights were off in the theatre. Jasmine knew that since The Lyric was a non-profit now, they had a stringent budget. She followed the light coming from behind the ticket booth, the administrative offices. There, she found her mother Donna seated at an enormous vintage desk pouring over books and entering numbers on a spreadsheet in a tablet.

“Good morning baby!” Donna greeted warmly.

“Morning mom! Looks like I’m interrupting?” Jasmine asked and passed her mother a latte.

“Oh no, no. I’m just adjusting our budget. We had to cut a couple of performances so we’ll have to cut some corners until the Christmas show. Thanks for the coffee honey.”

“Do you know what they’re performing for the holidays this year?” Jasmine perched on the edge of the grand desk. She wondered who used this office in the theatre’s glory days.

“I think they’re doing a Christmas Carol.” Donna made a few final entries on her spreadsheet and turned to Jasmine. “What are you up to today, sweetheart?”

"Well, not working," she frowned. "I think next year we need to close for the festival. I don't think I've had 5 appointments all week. Otherwise, who knows? I need to find an outfit for tomorrow. Maybe go check on my house?" Jasmine thought aloud.

"That's a good idea. Eric said he hadn't seen anything unusual when he drove by there yesterday."

"Eric?" Jasmine asked with surprise. "You talked to Eric?"

"Oh sure, he stopped by here yesterday with a basket of apples for me," Donna replied with a grin.

"That was thoughtful of him." Jasmine smiled. At least one of them had remembered about the apples. "What else did he say?"

"Oh, he was only here for a minute. Don't you worry I didn't get out the baby pictures. Yet." Donna teased.

"Well, that's a relief." Jasmine chuckled and hopped down from the desk. "I suppose I should go get ready for my only appointment of the day."

"Okay sweetie, I'll see you later." Donna turned back to her books.

Once outside, Jasmine grabbed her phone from a pocket and punched out a text with one hand.

"Talked to Mark Fitzgerald. Says he's in the process of selling that car to Vicki Andrews." She sent the message off to Detective Williams. Jasmine was certainly not experienced in murder investigations, but she'd seen enough movies to know that they still needed some concrete evidence before they arrested Vicki. It may have been creepy to run around town in a hood and dark sunglasses watching people, but it wasn't illegal.

Jasmine still had some unresolved questions. Who was that watching when the Detective had brought Sam Day in for questioning? It didn't look like Vicki. And why hadn't they brought Vicki in? Williams had first mentioned her as a, "person of interest," almost a week ago. Jasmine also wondered if a handwriting match on the notes would be enough evidence to convict someone of murder. She suspected it would not.

Jasmine found Ellie in her place behind the desk when she returned to the office. "Good morning, Ellie. Great job on the window display. I love it." She said with a smile.

"Oh really? Thanks, I wasn't sure I should do apples instead of pumpkins but when Dr. Canton stopped by with that big bag of apples it sure seemed kismet." Ellie beamed.

"Eric stopped here, too? Where was I?" Jasmine inquired.

"Oh, I think you'd gone for the day. It was kind of late, after 5," Ellie explained.

"Ah, I see. He does keep long hours. Well, I wanted to let you know you did an amazing job. Thanks for taking care of that."

"My pleasure boss."

When Jasmine returned to her office, Francis hardly looked up from his usual napping position. It was nearing 9:30. She sat down and checked her phone for messages. Nothing. She flipped to Google and did a few searches on handwriting as evidence to pass time while she waited for 10 am to arrive. As she'd suspected, handwriting matches alone rarely stood up in court. They would need something more substantial, like Molly Stephens' missing hairbrush, or even Lily Day's EpiPen.

Finally, it was almost 10 and Jasmine got into her lab coat. She found the halls of the clinic quite empty, maybe everyone else was as tired of waiting around as she was. She found Mr. Connelly and his full-sized senior poodle Priscilla in exam room four.

"Good morning Mr. Connelly." She greeted the pair. "How are you both doing today?"

"Well, I'm doing fine but I'm worried about Priscilla's tooth." Mr. Connelly replied.

"Oh? What's got you concerned?" Jasmine crouched to the dog's level, clicked on a bright light, and coaxed the dog to open her mouth. Priscilla was 11, it would be normal to have some dental issues at her age.

"Well her breath has gotten just terrible, and she won't eat hard foods anymore. Doesn't like her chew toys, either," he answered.

Jasmine got as good a look as she could at the dog's teeth. There did seem to be some decay and a back molar looked inflamed.

"You know some decay is normal at Priscilla's age. I think the soft food is fine, but maybe just mix a little broth or water in her hard food. Sometimes too much soft food can cause digestive issues. It does look like one tooth is pretty irritated, her gums are swollen around it. I'd like to clean her teeth, and possibly pull that one. She'll need anesthesia for that. So there's the cost to consider."

"Oh, I don't care what it costs. Can you do it today?" Mr. Connelly asked.

"Unfortunately I don't have the staff for a surgical procedure today, but I could get her in on Monday. In the meantime, I'll send you with something to bring down the swelling and ease any discomfort she might be feeling."

"Okay, great." He stroked Priscilla's head lovingly. Jasmine wrote out a prescription and took a deramaxx sample packet from a drawer. She wrapped the chewable in a soft treat.

"You can give her these, one in the morning, and one before bed, around every 12 hours. You can give them to her plain but I find most dogs need a treat to eat them." Jasmine offered the treat to Priscilla and the dog took it gently from her hand. Jasmine gave her a pat.

"Does any particular time work for you on Monday?" she asked.

"The sooner the better, I don't like to think she's in pain." He replied.

"I understand. The medicine really will ease that. You'll notice she sleeps a bit more than usual and that's totally normal. If she stops eating or has any other issues, call our 24 hour line." Jasmine knew Priscilla was going to be alright but she understood his concern. No one likes to see their pet uncomfortable.

She said her goodbyes to them both and scheduled the procedure with Ellie. Once in her office, Jasmine checked her cell phone again. This time she had 3 messages. One from Claire. "I think I'll skip work today, no appointments. I'll take the emergency calls." That was good news. They had a 24 hour line to serve as sort of a veterinary emergency room and they took turns taking those calls. They didn't get many calls but when there was an emergency, it was a vital service.

The other messages were from Eric. A sweet good morning, and an artful picture of a field full of sheep. Jasmine smiled for a selfie and added a good morning before she sent it to him. She clipped Francis to his leash and gave him a once over. His stitches could come out today. She led him to exam 1. She could probably lift him but didn't want to hurt him or herself. She stood back and tapped one finger on her chin. She didn't think Ellie would be much help when it came to lifting. Francis weighed more than 80 lbs.

On a whim, she said, "Up!" Much to her surprise, he leapt onto the table. She had to catch him, he jumped with so much enthusiasm, he nearly slid off the other side. She wrapped him in her arms and was rewarded with a series of wet kisses.

Jasmine delicately snipped the few stitches and pulled them out one at a time. Francis didn't flinch, though she had to dodge his tongue while she worked. She swabbed some antibacterial ointment over the cut and placed a small strip of tape over it. It was mostly healed, but she didn't want Francis to lick it while it finished healing. He licked her face again and she laughed.

"What am I going to do with you, huh?" She asked him. He cocked his head as if he didn't know what she could be talking about. It had been a few days since he'd been on the news with her, and that story had been shared all over social media thanks to Claire and the rest of her friends. If his owner was looking for him, surely they'd have been in touch by now. She smushed his face with both hands and gave him a good pet.

"Come on boy." She called and Francis jumped down as easily as he'd jumped up. Jasmine made a mental note; she would have to build a tall fence if she wanted to let him out without a leash. She took him out into the dog run for a few minutes and then they paid a visit to Ellie, who lapped up Francis' affections.

"I think we'll close for the day, El," Jasmine announced. Ellie lit up.

"Really? That's great! So many of my friends are in town, I can go meet up with everyone!" She practically cheered which made Jasmine smile.

"You know you can ask for time off any time, right?" Jasmine asked.

"Well sure, but I don't want to leave you guys shorthanded." Ellie switched off the computer and gathered up her school books. "Who should I forward the 24 hour line to?" she asked.

"Claire, please," Jasmine answered. "Have fun with your friends - maybe I'll see you at the fair tomorrow." She didn't want to hold Ellie up, she was positively buzzing with excitement. Jasmine flipped the sign on the door to closed. She collected her things and locked up.

Jasmine decided to go check on her house and pick up some fresh clothes. She caught a glimpse of the burgeoning fall fair setting up as she turned toward home. Ellie wasn't the only one excited about the weekend activities. She was especially thrilled about her date with Eric tomorrow night, but she was also looking forward to visiting all the animals at the fair, and of course, she was looking forward to shopping at all the booths. There would be hand-crafted goods and food from the whole area. Handspun wool clothes, candles, old fashioned soaps, beaded jewelry, locally canned preserves, you name it. Jasmine could hardly wait to wander through them all.

She and Francis arrived home. Jasmine gave the house a once over from the outside, and nothing seemed out of place except she would need to rake her yard before the neighbors started to complain. As they climbed the stairs up to the front door, she felt her stomach knot. There could be another creepy note waiting for her inside. There could even be a pile of them.

Jasmine sighed with relief as the door swung open. There were no ominous notes, in fact, there was no mail at all. She hung up her coat and Francis' leash and locked the door behind them. She stepped out of her tall boots and crept through her own house, checking all the rooms and windows, just in case. Everything seemed to be in place. She unpacked her overnight bag, dropping everything in the laundry bin. She laid it back out on her bed and packed for the weekend. She intended to come back home Monday, murder investigation or not.

She packed a little makeup and chose a cute outfit for tomorrow night. Once she was satisfied that she was prepared for tomorrow, she peeled out of her work clothes and slid into some warm running gear. She stepped into her trail runners. Today, Jasmine was going to tackle that muddy and more difficult trail. She wanted the challenge, but she was also hoping to gain some insight as to why Vicki Andrews had been on that trail hours after Lily Day had turned up dead.

Jasmine dug around in the junk drawer near the back door. She pulled out a sturdy canvas belt. It was meant to hold a water pack and other necessities during extended runs, but today she used it to clip Francis to herself. She planned to take him with her and she wanted her arms free but she still wasn't sure he wouldn't run off on his own. She took out a longer lead, looped one end around the canvas belt, and clipped it to Francis' collar.

She decided to skip the music today. A quick stretch and they hit the trail together. She set a slower, steady pace. She knew it would take a little extra effort to tackle that hill. It was not paved like the trail she ran most days, and it had rained only a few days ago. The mud may be slick, and there may be roots, rocks, and puddles to navigate. Jasmine hit her groove and listened to her breath which took on a lyrical rhythm. Francis kept up easily and Jasmine was grateful to whoever had taught the big fellow to heel. He stayed right at her side which was good news. At his size, he would easily yank Jasmine along if he wanted. She hoped he didn't like squirrels.

She saw lots of tourists along the trail which was comforting. Not a grey hoodie among them. When she reached the entrance to that intense trail, she turned heel onto it without hesitation. For the first time, Jasmine noticed a weathered sign which read, "Trapper's Trail." She was relieved to find it wasn't as muddy as she anticipated. There were a few small puddles and plenty of roots to dodge or bounce off of, but the path itself wasn't too slick. Still, she paced herself, as this trail had a steady incline.

Francis seemed to love this muddy terrain, he appeared to aim for the puddles rather than over or around them. Jasmine chuckled as he splashed into one. She was pleased she had taped over his cut earlier. Silly dog.

They'd been running on Trapper's Trail for about 15 minutes when the trail forked. Jasmine paused at the fork. Which way would Vicki have gone, she wondered. One side seemed to be lesser traveled than the other. The footpath was narrower and the foliage more overgrown. She was about to venture up that way when she felt a mighty yank and her waist. Francis was desperate to get at something just up the hill on the other trail. At first, she thought perhaps it was a dreaded squirrel, but then Jasmine caught sight of something shiny reflecting the soft October sun. She took Francis' lead in one hand so he couldn't pull her over and moved in for a closer look.

There at the base of an ancient white pine, something gleamed a brilliant silver. Francis struggled against the lead, clearly, the dog wanted desperately to dig the item up. But if it was what Jasmine thought it was, she didn't want him to disturb the scene more than the rain already had. She surveyed the trail around them and found a long stick. She grabbed it with her free hand and said, "Sit! Stay!" to Francis. He surprised her and obliged. She poked at the loose earth around the silver item until the mud gave way and it popped all the way out.

There it was. A silver-handled hairbrush. Jasmine tossed the stick and whipped out her phone. She snapped a couple of photos and then flipped through her other pictures. She found the picture of a handheld mirror she'd snapped in Molly Stephens' bedroom. The pattern matched.

There was only one reason for this hairbrush to be buried on a seldom traveled hiking trail. Jasmine had just found the murder weapon.

She took a few more pictures, then she flipped to Detective Williams' contact in her phone. She attached the photos and hit send before dialing the detective directly. Jasmine could hear her own heart pounding in her chest as the phone rang for what seemed like forever. Finally, someone picked up.

"Hello? Detective Williams?" it came out more panicked than Jasmine had planned.

"Yes. Jasmine? What's wrong?"

"Well nothing is wrong but you'd better get on your running shoes. I need you to meet me at the fork in Trapper's Trail as soon as possible. I think I found our murder weapon." The words hard hardly escaped her lips when Francis gave a low menacing growl down the hill. Jasmine heard a branch crack and turned to see a dark grey hood and pale face, this time without the sunglasses.

Vicki Andrews.

Jasmine could hear Detective Williams calling her name as she shoved the phone back in her pocket and turned tail to run up the overgrown path. There was no time to let the detective know what was going on, but Jasmine knew she'd given enough information for Williams to know where she was. She just hoped the detective hurried, because she had no idea where this trail went. It might loop around on itself as many hiking trails did. It was possible, however, that it just dead-ended somewhere deep in the woods.

Either way, she wasn't planning to stop running, because Vicki Andrews was hot on her heels behind her.

Jasmine was fast. She'd been running for years and she loved to run on trails much like this one. But she was traveling an unknown trail, uphill. Vicki seemed to be gaining on her. The actress had been on this trail before, and she was a lighter woman.

She also seemed to be driven by a wild rage. When Jasmine dared to sneak a look behind her, Vicki's hood had dropped away and her hair was flailing frantically around her. Her eyes were glazed over with hate. Jasmine heaved for air and tried to pick up her pace. Her nightmare about being chased by the mysterious hooded figure without a face had come to life.

They came to a small clearing and Jasmine saw a large branch. She crouched to swoop up the branch and swung around to face Vicki. She held the branch up like a baseball bat.

"Vicki stop! I don't want to hurt you." Jasmine felt Francis pulling at snarling at her side. Vicki did stop but she looked like she might pounce at any moment.

"Hurt me? You don't have the guts." She sneered. Jasmine stepped forward like she had every intention of slugging Vicki with that big branch.

"Try me." Jasmine's resolve surprised even herself. "What are you going to do, kill me out here in the woods? The police are already on their way, you'll be caught, and then what? You'll go down for two murders." She was just stalling, she didn't want to end up in a brawl with a crazy woman out her in the woods.

"All because of YOU! Why couldn't you leave it alone? None of this has anything to do with you. If you'd just kept your nose out and minded your own business, I'd be with Sam right now." Vicki spat out.

"You can't possibly believe that, Vicki. Sam loved Lily. You can't believe he'd just forget about her after YOU killed her." Jasmine reasoned.

"Doctor Cline!" Someone yelled from the trail behind Vicki. Jasmine glanced up and yelled back.

"Out here!"

In the seconds while Jasmine was looking away Vicki took the opportunity to leap at her. They both toppled over and Vicki struggled to get her hands around Jasmine's throat. Francis roared as the women tussled on the forest floor. Jasmine kneed the actress in the stomach and slid out from under her. She swiftly unclipped her utility belt, effectively freeing the angry dog. Francis grabbed the hood of Vicki's jacket in his powerful teeth and dragged her away from Jasmine.

By the time Jasmine was on her feet, Francis had Vicki pinned. She was lying on her back with her hands up. Francis hadn't bitten her, but he was standing, all fours on her chest, snarling an inch from her face. Jasmine moved to grab the lead.

"Dr. Cline!" Detective Williams huffed from the edge of the trail. She was flanked by several uniformed officers, all with guns drawn. They took aim for Vicki Andrews as Jasmine pulled Francis away from her. "You okay?" Detective Williams asked Jasmine.

"I am now," Jasmine responded. She crouched to whisper to Francis. She stroked him and calmed him back down. He had been such a good protector and he hadn't even harmed Vicki in the process. "Good boy." She whispered to him over and over.

Jasmine watched as the officers patted Vicki Andrews down and handcuffed her. She thought she heard one beginning to read Vicki her rights as they disappeared down the trail. Detective Williams nodded for Jasmine to join her and together they began the gradual descent down Trapper's Trail.

"That's quite a guard dog you've got there." Williams gestured to Francis.

"I'm so lucky he was here." Jasmine felt her pulse returning to normal.

"Agreed. You sure gave us all a good workout today. I've never seen half those boys run before." Williams chuckled.

"Well, it's important to get your exercise." Jasmine smiled. "Thanks for getting here so fast." The Detective nodded. They had reached the fork in the trail. That young man with the camera was there, taking photos as he had at the Lyric theatre nearly a week ago. A couple of other officers were standing around, one stood at the ready with an evidence bag.

"Try to wrap up here quickly," was all Williams said as they strode by. "I don't suppose I want to know what possessed you to come looking for a hairbrush in the forest. Do I?"

"That Sunday, the morning after Lily's death, I ran the main trail. I saw Vicki run up this way and it struck me as odd since it's such a hard trail. I just followed my gut." Jasmine confessed.

"Well, your gut just solved this case. I appreciate all your efforts but I hope you see now what I mean about the danger involved." Williams scolded, but gently.

"I do," Jasmine admitted, honestly. Perhaps she should have called the Detective before she went out to the woods, rather than after. Of course, she never could have guessed the murder weapon would be buried on the trail. "So, what happens now?"

"Now, we take Vicki into custody. Hopefully, we'll get a confession out of her. We'll search her house and that car she's been driving around, and with any luck, we will lock her up for a long, long time." Detective Williams explained. "Oh, and we'll release Sam Day."

"That's good news! When do you think that will happen?" Jasmine would like to stop and see him again.

"Just as soon as I get back to the station. And get all this muck off my boots." The Detective chuckled and smacked some mud off her boots. The two women shared a much needed laugh. They reached Jasmine's back stairs.

“I’ll need an official statement from you, too. I’ll give you a call to set that up. Thanks again, Jasmine.” Jasmine nodded and watched Detective Williams slip around the side of her house and out of sight.

Jasmine locked her back door behind herself and leaned heavily against it. She took some deep breaths and slid down the door to the floor. Francis nearly crawled in her lap and slurped her face. “Good boy.” She whispered again. Jasmine was thoroughly exhausted. The run itself had been challenging enough, but the adrenaline rush from being chased through the woods was wearing off. She grabbed a glass of water and poured some cool water into Francis’ bowl too.

Jasmine left a trail of running gear behind her on the way to the shower. She rinsed the mud and grime off as quickly as she could. She didn’t care that it was only 4 pm. She dressed for bed and sent Moira a text to let her know she was safe at home and not to worry.

Jasmine was asleep almost before the phone hit her nightstand.

CHAPTER FOURTEEN

Jasmine's weekend playlist woke her up bright and early Saturday morning. She heard someone belting out, "It's your thing, do what you wanna do," and she opened her eyes. She gave a big stretch and yawned. She sat up and found Francis sound asleep at the bottom of her bed.

As far as Jasmine was concerned, Francis could sleep anywhere he wanted. She patted his head and made the bed around him. She bopped around to the music and got ready for her day. It was Saturday and she had every reason to be in a fantastic mood. The Festival of Leaves Fair was today. She had a date with Eric later. And of course, Vicki Andrews was locked safely up down at the county jail. Jasmine no longer needed to look over her shoulder for hooded stalkers or wait until the next creepy note arrived.

Jasmine clipped Francis to his leash and slipped out the backdoor. From the edge of her yard opposite the trail, they had a perfect view of the sunrise over the valley. She pulled up a stump as a seat and Francis sat beside her. The sky was already a pleasant peach hue. Together they watched as the peach turned pink and the sky lit up as the sun crept over the edge of the valley. Jasmine looked away just as the sun came into view and tugged Francis away.

"Beautiful, huh? Still, sunsets are my favorite." Francis woofed and Jasmine decided he agreed.

She happily unpacked her overnight bag. Staying with Moira had been lovely but Jasmine was delighted to be able to sleep in her own bed and settle back into her routine. She popped her dirty clothes in the washer and started a pot of coffee. She poured Francis a little extra kibble. He had burned some serious calories yesterday. Come to think of it, so had she. Jasmine whipped up some apple cinnamon pancakes and scrambled eggs to go with her coffee. She sat down to enjoy them and send Eric a cheery good morning text.

She took time getting dressed. She wanted to look nice when she saw Eric later, but she also wanted to be comfortable and warm at the fair all day. She settled on a fitted black cowl neck sweater and pale denim leggings. She switched out her tall riding style boots for a more delicate looking pair in black leather.

She smoothed her curls into a low pony and did some subtle makeup. Berry lip stain, a little mascara, and eye shadow. Satisfied with her look, Jasmine took out a cream color wool coat. Though the sun was shining, she knew full well that it would be chilly outdoors all day in mid-October.

She and Francis loaded up in the car by 10 am. Jasmine wanted ample time to explore all the stalls and displays at the fair, and she had an errand she wanted to run first. As she arrived on Grand Avenue, the street was bustling with activity. She decided to use her parking spot behind the animal clinic. She left Francis behind for a few minutes to take care of that errand.

When Jasmine arrived at Blackbird, a few people were already inside shopping for one-of-a-kind clothing and accessories. Moira Randall was perched in her usual spot on the desk. She was wearing a jet black tea dress with leather detailing at the shoulders and a dramatic red petticoat. The dress was belted with a thin red patent leather belt and flattered Moira's curves to perfection. Jasmine smiled as Moira waved her over.

"Well, good morning stranger! If it isn't the town hero! I heard you had quite a day yesterday." Moira announced.

"You heard about that?" Jasmine asked.

"Oh honey, everybody's heard about that. Small towns." Moira clicked her tongue. "How are you feeling after all that?"

"I feel fantastic." Jasmine wasn't exaggerating. "I wanted to thank you for inviting me to stay with you this week. You made a scary situation feel like a vacation."

"Aw Jazz. I'm happy to hear it. Come stay again sometime soon." Moira offered warmly.

"I will do that. Say, I wonder if you can order pieces for those vanity sets individually?" she asked.

"Yes, I think we can do that. How come? I should think you'd be happy never to see one again." Moira mused aloud.

"It's not for me." Jasmine chuckled. "I thought I could replace the missing pieces for Molly."

"Oh, that's kind of you. You remember which set?" Moira asked.

"Oh yeah, I have a picture," Jasmine answered.

"Send it to me and I'll get the order in Monday."

"Perfect, thanks. Really, Moira, thanks for everything." Jasmine squeezed her friend's hand.

"My pleasure, babe." Moira hopped down to help some customers and Jasmine hurried back to fetch Francis.

Jasmine and Francis enjoyed the stroll down Grand Avenue. People bustled by, talking and laughing, enjoying a lovely autumn day. They arrived at the entrance to the fair and Jasmine felt very much like she'd stepped back in time. It could easily have been the same harvest time festival Merritt Valley had hosted a hundred years ago. In the center, there was a small stage set up. Of course, it was empty this early in the day, as was the wooden platform which served as a dance floor. There were lights strung around it. Everywhere, bushels of dried corn leaves and pumpkins accented walkways.

There were rows and rows of vendor booths. Jasmine knew that behind the stage there were huge tents and a roped-off ring where cows and horses and even goats would be judged. School clubs like 4H and scouts had booths sprinkled throughout the aisles of vendors, along with local charitable organizations.

It was one such nonprofit that Jasmine wanted to visit, first. She wandered the rows with Francis until they came upon Precious Paws Rescue. She knew the young man sitting behind the table, he occasionally brought over a truckload of rescued cats and dogs for discounted shots, spay, and neutering.

“Good morning, Teddy.” Jasmine extended a hand.

“Oh, good morning Doctor Cline. Nice to see you.”

“It’s nice to see you, too. Say, I wondered if Francis and I might be of service, volunteering. He’s sort of small-town famous and I thought it might give adoptions a little boost.” Jasmine offered.

“That’s a great idea. Here fill out these forms.” Teddy pushed over a basic volunteer document and a form that a vet would fill out, verifying the pet volunteering has current vaccinations. “You know, he might even be of help, like, right now. Today.” Teddy suggested. A half dozen people were already nudging in close to ask if they could pet Francis, who wagged his tail eagerly.

“I thought he might.” Jasmine smiled. She and Francis hung around the booth for a couple of hours Francis performed his tricks for a few people and received free snuggles from nearly everyone who passed. Dozens of people stopped to chat with Teddy about adoption and pets currently available.

After a couple of hours, Jasmine was hungry and getting antsy to check out all the other booths.

“Hey, Teddy, would you mind watching Francis for a little while? I want to grab a bite and do a bit of shopping.”

“Oh yeah, I don’t mind at all. Take your time.” Teddy smiled. Jasmine felt confident leaving Francis in his capable hands.

Her first stop was at a food stand where she got a piece of corn on the cob on a stick. It was simply dripping with butter. Her first bite took her straight back to high school. She'd had corn on the cob at this fair every year growing up. She nibbled on it as she walked the rows, stopping to admire elaborate landscapes painted on antique saw blades and lawn sculptures made of repurposed tractor parts.

A twinkle of rainbow color glass pieces caught her eye and she stopped at a booth filled with handcrafted jewelry. A chat with the gentleman manning the booth informed her that he was a retired diesel mechanic. After decades working on tractors and combines, he had found a hobby twining recycled copper around natural stones and glass beads. The pieces were delicate and lovely. Jasmine picked out one for herself and Moira. Moira's was in vivid jewel tones, while those she chose for herself and her mother were more muted natural tones.

Jasmine also made stops at a local soap maker's booth. She took her time sniffing all the gorgeous hand-cut soaps. Some had bits of lavender or oats blended right into the bar. She had trouble deciding which ones to try and left that booth with an armload of soaps. She admired the carved furnishings at another booth, though they weren't at all her style.

Jasmine was drawn in again when she came to a small purple tent with bits of mirrored glass swinging from its tassels. As she entered the tent, she felt like she might encounter gypsy's who would read her fortune. Instead, she found stacks and stacks of felted wool socks, hats, scarves, and mittens. She ran her hand over a few and chose some thick woolen socks in cream and chestnut.

When she finally returned to the Precious Paws Booth, her arms were laden with goodies. She was beaming, Jasmine just loved to search out unique items, and supporting local artists made it even more special. She returned to the booth to find a crowd had gathered. She snuck around them to find Eric there in the middle, putting on a show with Francis.

"Up!" Eric called out and raised his arm higher than Jasmine could reach. Francis leapt up and took a treat from Eric and the small crowd cheered. Eric got Francis to sit, speak, high five and rollover. The kids seemed especially delighted. Francis was happy to have the attention and treats. Eric beamed.

"Thanks, everyone! Remember to adopt, don't shop!" Eric gave a little bow. The crowd dispersed. A few kids stayed behind to snap shots of Francis and give him a pet. Eric laughed when he saw Jasmine and her armloads of shopping bags. He reached out and plucked them from her arms.

"I guess everyone can close up shop. Looks like you cleaned the place out." He joked. He bent to kiss her cheek and Jasmine giggled.

"Oh come on. I left a couple of things behind." Jasmine laughed.

"Only a couple. Come on we can drop these off, my truck is just back here." They left Francis with Teddy and took the only path Jasmine hadn't traveled today, the one which led to the farm tents and horse ring. Jasmine could see some riders jumping barrels in the ring as they passed. Eric set all her bags gently in the cab of his truck.

"Come on I'll introduce you." Eric grinned and captured her hand. They ambled through the stables and Eric stopped to chat with almost everyone they saw. He made introductions each time and explained their farm or breed specialty. Jasmine had some knowledge of farming and even animal husbandry, but she struggled to keep up with it all.

They stopped to see the kids at one stall. Eric picked one up and handed it to her. The little creature snuggled right in. He was so sweet Jasmine found herself cooing to the little guy, and looked up to catch Eric snapping a picture of her.

"Goodness, I just can't escape cameras this week!" Jasmine exclaimed.

"Well, you can't blame me. Just look at you." Eric showed her the picture. It was a lovely shot. She turned to feign annoyance again, but before she could say a word, Eric kissed her, and the world fell away. She was just floating in space, kissing him. The baby goat in her arms bleated. It startled them both and they laughed.

They spent the afternoon visiting stalls, feeding babies, and once in a while, Eric was drawn away with work. Jasmine was happy to visit with the animals or make small talk with farmers. She understood the appeal of this life. Farm folk worked hard but there were so many rewards. She wondered if one day she might join them.

She thought they had seen everyone when Eric led her to a separate structure just outside the horse ring. She thought she recognized the laughter inside, and then a familiar white dog peeked out of a stall.

"Clyde!" Jasmine called. Once inside she gave the great Pyrenees and good scratch behind the ears. She looked up to find Sarah and Chris Benton, Sarah's little brother Ben was not far behind them.

"Jasmine!" Sarah called. She ran over and gave Jasmine a solid hug. I heard all about you and that Vicki Andrews! I'm so glad you're okay." Sarah huffed.

"Oh, it wasn't that big of a deal," Jasmine said.

"I don't know, I think wrestling with a psycho is sort of a big deal, especially in Merritt." Chris chimed in. Jasmine shrugged. She was desperate to change the subject.

"Hey, how's Apollo?" Eric asked, seeming to read her mind.

"He's doing great, come one, he's right back here with Apollonia." Chris lead them to a roped-off area behind the temporary stables. Apollonia trotted around in a circle and little Apollo appeared from behind his mother. He was already nearly as tall as Jasmine and full of personality.

"May I?" Jasmine asked. Chris and Sarah both nodded and Jasmine reached out to touch the little colt. He shook his mane and ran the circle again. Jasmine giggled. "Goodness, he's cute."

"Almost as cute as our little guy will be," Chris said softly. Jasmine turned around. Oh, Sarah, you're?" She left the question open.

"That's right we're expecting." Sarah glowed.

"Oh my God, that's wonderful! Congratulations!" Jasmine exclaimed. She gave Sarah another hug.

"Hey, congrats!" Eric said and shook Chris' hand. Sarah and Jasmine exchanged looks and laughed. "What?" Eric asked, clueless. The women laughed again.

Jasmine and Eric enjoyed a visit with the Bentons and met several other horses. When they parted ways Jasmine left with a promise to come riding with Sarah next week.

"Should we find something to eat?" Eric asked.

"Yes please, I'm starved," Jasmine replied.

"Me too," Eric answered. They made their way back to the fair. They were trying to decide what to eat when Jasmine heard a familiar voice behind her.

"Doctor Cline." Detective Williams said.

"Oh hi, Detective Williams," Jasmine answered.

"Hello," Eric added. The Detective nodded.

"I'm pleased to see you up and about. It occurred to me after I left yesterday, we ought to have had a paramedic look you over." Williams said flatly.

"Oh no, I'm alright," Jasmine assured, though the detective was probably right. "I do hope you're not ready to take my statement right now though, I'm sort of in the middle of things."

"No, no. That can wait until Monday. I just wanted to say hello… and" Williams glanced around surveying the crowd, "I wanted to let you know about a couple of things my team has discovered since last night." Williams flashed Eric a look.

"Why don't I go get us some gyros." Eric offered. He took a hint well.

"I wanted to tell you that we found an EpiPen prescribed to one Lily Day in the glovebox of Vicki's car." Williams confided when they were alone.

"Oh, that's good news. Wow. That means I was right." Jasmine said offhand.

"From the very beginning. There's something else, too." Williams began.

"What's that?" Jasmine encouraged.

"We found facial prosthetics in her home." Williams finished.

"Facial prosthetics? Like fake noses?" Jasmine was perplexed. Detective Williams chuckled wryly.

"Exactly like that. Silicone noses, cheeks, chins, things like that. Turns out Vicki Andrews is an expert in effects makeup."

"Oh wow. That means that was her, that day. I caught her spying on Sam when you picked him up for questioning." Jasmine processed her thoughts out loud.

"That's right," Williams replied.

"Good. I wondered about that."

"So did I. But that mystery is also solved. We found drafts of those poems all over Vicki's house, too. Looks like an open and shut case."

"That's such good news!" Jasmine resisted the urge to jump up and down. She was so overjoyed and relieved. The case was closed, and there were no loose ends to worry about.

"I thought so. I wanted to deliver that news in person. I hope you won't mind if I downplay your role in the investigation. Unless you want to dodge Nancy Vale and the others the next few months." Williams chuckled again.

"Lord no. I don't mind at all." Jasmine smiled.

"I'm glad. I'll get in touch Monday about your statement. Better get back to your date. He's hot." The Detective said and disappeared as swiftly as she had appeared.

Jasmine found Eric chatting with the ladies at the gyro truck. He passed her a Gyro and they found a small table amid the trucks. Jasmine took a hearty bite of her Gyro. She closed her eyes to enjoy the smokey meat and feta cheese wrapped in light pita bread. She opened her eyes to find Eric watching her intently. She felt herself flush.

"What?" she asked, embarrassed.

"I just think you're the cutest thing I've seen in my whole life." Eric grinned.

"Oh stop that. You see cute things every day." Jasmine tried to play off his sweet compliment. She couldn't stop blushing.

"True. My statement stands." They enjoyed their meal and sipped pink lemonade. "Hey what did the detective want, anyway?" Eric asked when he'd finished his gyro.

"She just wanted to tell me things are going well in the case. They found lots of evidence. It was good news." Jasmine answered.

"You did some great work on this, Jazz," Eric said, sincerely. "But maybe you could avoid murderers for a while. For me? It's no good for my heart." There was concern in his voice.

"I'll do my best to avoid anything like this, I promise." Jasmine was rather looking forward to settling back into her life as a small-town vet, sans the crazy murderous stalker.

"Good. Now I have a very important question for you." Eric said seriously. Jasmine cocked her head, much like Francis did when she said silly things to him.

"Can you show me where to get some of those good smelly soaps? That bag smelled amazing." He stifled a laugh.

"Good smelly soaps, huh? Is that the technical phrase?" They laughed together. "Sure, come on." They tossed their trash and stopped by the Precious Paws booth. It looked like Teddy was getting ready to wrap up for the day.

"Thanks so much for watching Francis all day," Jasmine said and fetched Francis.

"Oh he's been great company, it was my pleasure. Have fun tonight!" Teddy called after them.

Eric and Jasmine wandered around with Francis, chatting with artists and old friends visiting for the festival. Eric did pick up some homemade soaps and even a pair of sturdy wool socks for the impending winter. They laughed and talked and tried on silly hats. They even shared some cotton candy. Together, they wandered the fair until the booths started to close down and the sunset. The twinkly lights came on at dusk and Jasmine could hear the first band begin to play.

"Hey, why don't I go drop off Francis at the Benton's stable? Clyde can babysit." Eric offered with a smile. Jasmine nodded and passed him Francis's lead. Eric bent down and planted a small soft kiss on her cheek. She watched as he sauntered off toward the farm tents.

"Well, that's a pleasant view." Moira's pleasant voice teased.

"Oh stop that," Jasmine said. "How are you?"

"I'm doing great, though I think perhaps, not quite as well as you. Having fun?"

"I really am. Today has been just… perfect." Jasmine couldn't stop smiling if she'd wanted to. She didn't.

"Hey let's go check out the band," Moira suggested. Together they made their way to the stage. People were gathering under the strings of lights. The band was local and small, but talented. It wasn't long at all before a few people were out on the dance floor. Moira included. A handsome fellow Jasmine didn't recognize stopped by and took her friend's hand and she had swirled away. Moira was a good dancer and her red petticoat was made for dancing.

Jasmine watched Moira and the others dance and when the songs switched, found her being pulled onto the dance floor. She and Moira laughed and danced through a couple of songs and when the music stopped she found that Eric was watching her. She wandered over to him as the band started up again. As if on cue, they played a slower song. Eric took her hands in his.

"I think I promised you a dance." He whispered.

"I believe that you did." Jasmine agreed. He twirled her out onto the dance floor. She laughed and they danced easily together.

"Oh, you really can dance," Jasmine mentioned.

"I told you I could. I could get used to this." Eric said.

"Used to what?" Jasmine asked.

"Having you in my arms," Eric answered. Jasmine blushed. "Though, maybe wear heels." It was a bit of a stretch for her to reach his shoulders.

"That's a good idea. Next time? Are you planning to take me out dancing again?" Jasmine asked with a smile.

"Definitely." Eric smiled but his tone was serious. They turned and danced in the other direction. Jasmine was vaguely aware that much of the crowd was watching them.

"You know, there aren't many places to go dancing in Merritt." Jasmine mused.

"True. But there's the Festival next year."

"That's a whole year away, Eric." Jasmine gazed into his endless blue eyes. They twinkled like the strings of lights around them.

"Mhm." Eric kissed her softly.

"You want to take me out next year?" Jasmine asked again.

"Mhm," was all he said, and he kissed her again.

Perhaps they were rushing into things. She didn't care. She reached up and kissed him again. She felt him smile and they laughed together. The music came to a stop and Jasmine realized that had been their first dance.

It wouldn't be their last.

The End

Made in the USA
Coppell, TX
02 December 2021

66895750R20125